El Salvador

Beauty Among the Ashes

by Faith Adams

Dillon Press, Inc.   Minneapolis, Minnesota 55415

The photographs are reproduced through the courtesy of Jean Boller; the Central America Resource Center; Eugene V. Harris (1913-1978) and the Eugene Harris Slide Library; Michael Kennedy; Gerald Lacey; Ione Mabrey; Nancy Olive; Jackie Solem; and Don Yager. Cover: a Salvadoran girl (Eugene Harris Slide Library).

Library of Congress Cataloging in Publication Data

Adams, Faith.
    El Salvador: beauty among the ashes.

    Bibliography:
    Includes index.
    Summary: Describes the people, history, folklore, social life, and customs of the Central American country and examines the plight of those Salvadorans who have fled their war-torn land to take refuge in the United States.
    1. El Salvador—Juvenile literature. 2. Salvadorans—United States—Juvenile literature. [1. El Salvador. 2. Salvadorans—United States] I. Title.
    F1483.2.A34   1985   972.84   85-6945
    ISBN 0-87518-309-3

Dillon Press, Inc., 242 Portland Avenue South
Minneapolis, Minnesota 55415

Printed in the United States of America
1 2 3 4 5 6 7 8 9 10 93 92 91 90 89 88 87 86

Contents

Preface

Any mention of El Salvador these days is likely to lead
to a discussion charged with emotion. Every aspect of
the conflict, from the plight of the refugees and the
sanctuary movement, to the funding of the Salvadoran
military, is controversial.

For most Americans, the discussions revolve around
newspaper headlines and television reports. An understanding of Salvadoran history, and the U.S. role in it, is
often absent. This book discusses various areas of Salvadoran life, from school life and family life, to history
and culture, in the hope that it will aid the reader's
understanding and appreciation of El Salvador. Several
suggestions in "Central America: What U.S. Educators
Need to Know," *(Interracial Books for Children Bulletin*, Vol. 13, Nos. 2 & 3, 1982) were most helpful in this
regard. In particular, these articles highlighted issues
that are too often neglected in children's literature about
Central America and offered guidelines to educators
and writers desiring to inform young people more about
Central American countries.

This book seeks to give a representative view of life
in El Salvador. Giving an accurate representation of the
factions involved in the current conflict was a constant
challenge, but an attempt was made to present the position of all sides in a fair and straightforward way. It

is my hope that readers of this book, young as well as old, teacher as well as student, will learn something new about El Salvador. Above all, I hope that they will look beyond the headlines and the politics and try to understand the impact of the war on the people of this small, crowded, and bitterly divided Central American nation.

Fast Facts About El Salvador

Official Name: República de El Salvador.

Capital: San Salvador.

Location: Central America; Honduras lies to the north and east, Guatemala lies to the northwest, and the Pacific Ocean forms the coastline to the south.

Area: 8,260 square miles (21,393 square kilometers); the greatest distances are 163 miles (262 kilometers) from east to west and 88 miles (142 kilometers) from north to south. El Salvador has 189 miles (304 kilometers) of Pacific coastline. It is the smallest Central American country in area.

Elevation: *Highest:* Monte Cristo—7,933 feet (2,418 meters)

Lowest—sea level.

Population: 5,536,000 (1985 estimate)

Distribution: Urban—43% (1985 estimate)
Rural—57% (1985 estimate)

Density: 575 people per square mile (1980).

Land Distribution: 2 percent of the population own 57.5 percent of the land; 60 percent of rural peasants are landless.

Nutrition: 75 percent of children under the age of five are malnourished (sick because they don't eat enough of the right kinds of food); El Salvador has the lowest per capita consumption (amount eaten per person) of calories in Latin America.

Form of Government: Officially a democratic republic according to the present Constitution, adopted in 1983. Military leaders and wealthy landowners actually hold most of the political power. Since 1931, most of El Salvador's government leaders have been army officers.

Important Products: Coffee, cotton, shrimp, sugar; beverages, canned foods, organic fertilizers, cement, plastics.

Basic Unit of Money: Colón.

Major Languages: Spanish; Nahua, the Indian language, is spoken by a small number of people.

Major Religion: Roman Catholic.

Flag: Three horizontal stripes in blue, white, and blue.

National Anthem: *Saludemos La Patria Orgullosos* ("We Proudly Salute Our Country").

Major Holidays: New Year's Day—January 1; Easter; Independence Day—September 15; Christmas—December 25.

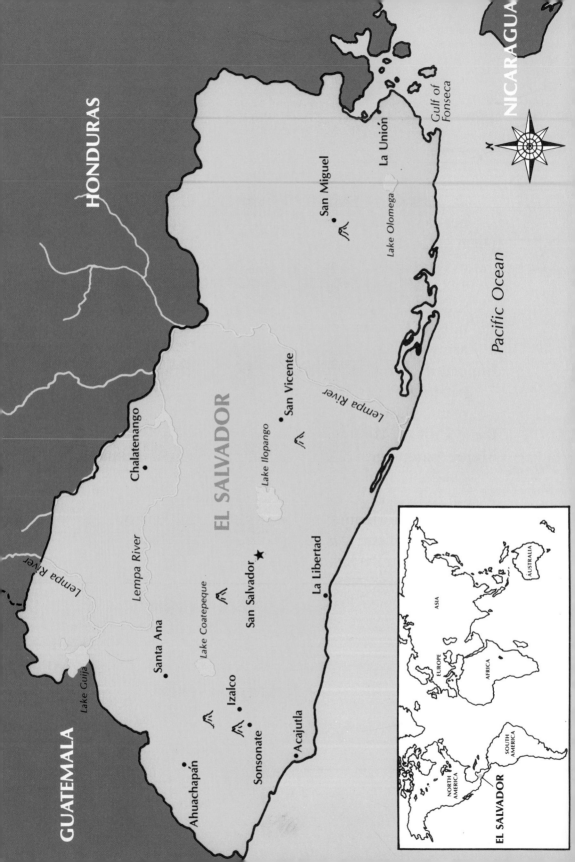

1. A Beautiful, War-Torn Land

El Salvador is made up of land and people as varied as the colors and designs in a Mayan Indian weaving. The blues and greens in the weaving could be the lakes and mountains of northwestern El Salvador. The reds and oranges look like the colors of a volcano when it erupts. The black thread holding the cloth together could be the hardworking people doing their daily tasks throughout El Salvador.

In the cool mountains of Chalatenango province, young children warm themselves around a crackling morning fire while their mother fetches water. A worker at the southern port of Acajutla wipes his sweaty brow as he helps load coffee onto a ship. In the capital city of San Salvador, a bank teller rides the bus downtown to the modern bank where she works. Out on the highway, a Coca-Cola truck passes a burro laden with firewood.

Although it's just 163 miles (262 kilometers) across at its widest point (or about the size of Massachusetts), El Salvador has everything from lakes and mountains to volcanoes and ocean beaches. It has centers of industry in big, modern cities. Surrounding the cities are coffee and sugar cane fields.

El Salvador is located in the center of the Western

Hemisphere. If you took a map of the Americas and folded North America over South America, the crease would fall on Central America, in the area of El Salvador In the past Central America has often been looked upon as if it were only a bridge between North America and South America. But Central America is an interesting and important part of the world, with its own traditions, ways of life, and current problems.

Honduras borders El Salvador on the north and east. Guatemala lies to the northwest. The Pacific Ocean provides the south coast with a beautiful stretch of black sand beaches. Nicaragua is to the southwest, across the Gulf of Fonseca.

A Land Divided

Although El Salvador is small, it is home to five million people. Because there are so many people living on so little land, every acre of land is precious. Coffee is planted on the slopes that rise up toward the country's numerous volcanoes.

A small number of people own most of the coffee fields in El Salvador. These few, extremely wealthy landowners earn about half of the nation's annual income. They own several homes in El Salvador, and some have houses in other countries. Most Salvadorans, though, are poor. Every day children die because

A Salvadoran farm worker harvests coffee beans.

they don't have enough of the right kinds of food to eat and clean water to drink.

Many of the poor people work in the coffee fields where they pick the coffee beans when they are red and ready for harvest. Some of the workers live near the fields. Others travel many miles to work during the few months of harvest, because jobs are hard to find.

Whether they are rich or poor, Salvadorans share a

fierce love for their beautiful land and loyalty towards their country. They disagree about how their country should be run, though. El Salvador is in the midst of a civil war—a revolution by one group of its people against those who have long ruled the nation. In many parts of the country, people live in constant fear for their lives. Since 1979, more than fifty thousand Salvadorans have been killed. Almost everyone has had friends or relatives killed or imprisoned because of the war.

Throughout the land, the government army is fighting against the guerrilla army. The government army is made up of soldiers who are defending El Salvador's present way of life. The guerrilla army is made up of farm workers, students, and others who want to change the country. The guerrillas want to give land to the farm workers who till the soil, reduce poverty and hunger, and provide better education and health care. This revolutionary group believes that it can improve the quality of life for most Salvadorans.

El Salvador—a nation with the beauty and variety of a Mayan weaving—is being unraveled for a time. Some Salvadorans want to hold on to the old, familiar pattern in the weaving. They want to keep the old, familiar way of life. Others want to weave an entirely new design from the old threads of the weaving. They want to change Salvadoran society. Each side thinks it is doing what is best for El Salvador.

An Indian Heritage

Most Salvadorans are mestizos—people of mixed European and American Indian ancestry who have shiny hair and dark skin and eyes. Some Salvadorans are Indian. Their ancestors were the first inhabitants of El Salvador. Other Salvadorans have white skin, light hair, and blue eyes. In the northern province of Chalatenango, many people have the fair complexions of their Spanish ancestors. Much of the upper class in El Salvador also has fair skin. The upper class is largely made up of people of English, French, or Spanish descent whose ancestors came to El Salvador from Europe within the last few hundred years.

The Indian background of the mestizo population can be traced back thousands of years. Nahua Indians lived in El Salvador as early as 3,000 B.C. Maya Indians built huge limestone pyramids in western El Salvador between A.D. 100 and 1000. Scientists called anthropologists and archeologists have studied the Mayan ruins at Tazumal, El Trapito, and San Andrés. They have some clues about the past of the Mayas, but there is much that we will never know about their civilization.

We do know that they were advanced in scientific thought, and that they respected nature above all else. The Mayas thought that the corn they planted and harvested was sacred. Corn is still an important part of the

Salvadoran diet. In fact, most Salvadorans eat corn tortillas every day. Much of the food that Salvadorans eat is similar to what the Mayas ate long ago.

In the 1520s, Spanish explorers arrived in Central America. They named one of the regions that they explored after Jesus the savior—*El Salvador*. Along with the Spanish language, the explorers brought the Catholic religion and European clothing and lifestyles. Today, centuries later, most areas in El Salvador have been more influenced by the Spaniards than by the Indians who first lived there.

But in the town of Izalco, some people still speak Nahua, an ancient Indian language. And in neighboring towns, Indian dress is still worn. The men wear white pants and shirts and broad-brimmed hats. Women wear long, full skirts and blouses. On their heads they carry baskets filled with fresh fruits and vegetables.

Tongues of Fire

Not far from Izalco is the volcano Izalco. It last erupted in the 1960s, spouting and smoking with great energy. The tongues of fire could be seen from the Pacific Ocean, twenty-five miles away. For that reason, the volcano was nicknamed "Lighthouse of the Pacific."

El Salvador has twenty-two volcanoes that form two rows and run from east to west across the country.

Like nine out of ten Salvadorans, this woman and her granddaughter are mestizos.

One of El Salvador's twenty-two volcanoes, Izalco is sometimes called "Lighthouse of the Pacific."

Each of the four main colonial cities—Santa Ana, San Vicente, San Miguel, and San Salvador—has a nearby volcano bearing the name of the town. Most of the volcanoes haven't erupted for a long time. Some produce steam, which bubbles up through the mud and sometimes makes a loud hiss. Other volcanoes heat nearby pools of water, which can become so hot that the water boils!

The ash from the volcanoes makes a fertile covering for the soil where the crops are grown. Coffee is El Salvador's most important export crop, and sugar cane and cotton are also shipped to foreign countries. Coffee and sugar cane fields surround the nation's three largest cities—San Salvador, Santa Ana, and San Miguel.

The "Holy Savior"

San Salvador means "Holy Savior" in Spanish. It lies among hills and valleys in an area called *Valle de Las Hamacas* ("Valley of the Hammocks") because of its gentle slopes. The land may look like hammocks, but the capital is not a restful place. Downtown San Salvador hums with activity. Buses rush through the narrow streets where many poor children, especially boys, work as vendors. They shine shoes, or sell chewing gum and newspapers. Some middle-class adults work in modern office buildings and shops.

Downtown San Salvador on a Saturday afternoon is a busy and crowded city center.

San Salvador has many new buildings. After earthquakes in 1854 and 1917 destroyed the city, it had to be rebuilt. In the heart of San Salvador are the National Palace, the Center of Government, Liberty Park, Rosario Church, and the Municipal Palace. In other parts of the city soccer fields and stadiums are often filled by cheering Salvadoran soccer fans.

Though San Salvador doesn't have a large number of parks, many children play at *Parque Infantíl* ("Children's Park"). They roller-skate in the big rink, holding on to their friends' hands and trying not to fall. They ride on the merry-go-round and drive little boats through the pond.

Another popular place in San Salvador is *El Reloj de Flores* ("The Clock of Flowers"). This giant clock made of flowers can be seen from far away. Of course the hands have to be mechanical in order to keep time!

To the west of downtown there are nice, modern homes in the suburbs, called *colonias.* Doctors, accountants, and well-to-do business people live in these fashionable areas. The east side of downtown has many slums, which are called *tugurios.* Thousands of people here live in houses made of cardboard or tin. These poor people might work as maids or in factories, or they might not work at all, because there aren't jobs for everyone.

In the countryside Salvadorans also have a hard time finding full-time jobs. Still, the people have work to do even if they aren't paid for it. Since they don't have running water, the women get up as early as five in the morning to fetch water. All day long they work hard. The women cook for their families, wash clothes, raise chickens or pigs, and sometimes tend gardens. Men try to get jobs working in the fields, planting and harvesting crops. Between these seasons they are often unemployed.

Even though the Salvadoran people don't have

Children in a tugurio *on the east side of San Salvador.*

much, they are generous with what they have. Salvadorans enjoy the company of friends and relatives. When guests come, they will be given a piece of cheese along with the usual beans, rice, and tortillas.

A Beautiful Land

Throughout the country, the land is as beautiful as the people are generous. On the drive from San Salvador west to Santa Ana, there is a giant stretch of lava rock from the volcano San Salvador. It's called *El Mar de Lava* ("The Sea of Lava"). Since the ground is black for miles, it's hard to tell where the highway ends and the lava rock begins.

Pine-covered mountains lie north of San Salvador. Here the land that isn't forest is used for grain crops and pasture for animals. In the mountains the higher altitude brings cooler temperatures that make a sweater or jacket feel good in the morning.

Geysers and hot springs in the western provinces of Ahuachapán and Sonsonate provide energy for many Salvadorans. In fact, the people use the boiling water from these hot springs to cook eggs! The government uses the heat from the water to produce electricity. Because of its geysers and dams, El Salvador doesn't have to import fuel for electric power plants.

In the country's green and tropical south coast region, palm trees, coconuts, tamarinds, watermelons, and mangoes grow abundantly. This area is even wet enough for rice fields.

Many beaches along the Pacific Ocean are covered with fine black sand darkened by volcanic activity throughout the country. Most Salvadoran children grow up thinking that all sand is black because they have never seen white sand! Salvadoran families like to go to the beach whenever they can. Easter is an especially popular time to go to the ocean. And since the weather is warm year-round, they can go at Christmas or in the middle of July.

Because El Salvador is quite near the equator, the sun rises and sets at approximately the same time of day in all seasons. The sun always rises between 5:00 and 5:30 A.M. and sets between 5:30 and 6:00 P.M. Salvadorans who work in the coffee fields can tell time by looking at the sky, and they seldom own watches or clocks. Instead, they read the sun as if it were a clock.

There are only two seasons in El Salvador, a dry season and a rainy season. During the rainy season, which lasts from May to October, it rains every day. Giant black clouds fill the sky during the late afternoon or evening. Soon the rains, called *temporales*, come down in sheets. The skies are clear by the next morning, and in the afternoon the cycle is repeated. The rainy season in El Salvador can wash out roads and cause floods.

The rain does help the crops grow and keeps El Salvador's three hundred rivers from drying up. The *Río Lempa* is El Salvador's most important river. From its source in Guatemala, it crosses a corner of Honduras, cuts across El Salvador's mountain range, and then flows to the Pacific.

The largest lakes in El Salvador are Lake Ilopango and Lake Coatepeque. Turtles and crocodiles live in the rivers, and colorful fish dart through the waters.

Lake Coatepeque is one of El Salvador's largest lakes.

Because so much land in El Salvador is cultivated, there are not a lot of wild animals in the countryside. Birds are the most beautiful wildlife. Wild ducks, white and royal herons, blue jays, and other bright-feathered birds perch in the trees. The urraca has a most unusual call. It sounds more like a human laugh than a bird call!

The quetzal was a rare bird that lived during the Mayan age. A striking green and deep red in color, the quetzal had patterns of gold and violet on its feathers. In the sunshine it reflected all the colors of the rainbow. The quetzal is extinct now, but its likeness is found on Mayan weavings. It is a reminder of El Salvador's majestic past.

2. Families, Faith, and Hope

Salvadorans are much like people everywhere, and yet, they have certain characteristics that make them distinctly Salvadoran. They share land, water, religion, food, and a common history. As a result, Salvadorans have a bond with each other that is stronger than the bond they have with people from other countries. These shared characteristics, among others, make up the Salvadoran culture, or way of life.

Places to Have Fun

One activity that most Salvadorans enjoy is getting together with friends and family. Big parties and dances are very popular among people of all ages. Even though they might not have much money, Salvadorans dress up and look handsome when they go out. If they go out for the evening, they often stay out very late. In the cities, especially, people sometimes leave home well past midnight to go to a nightclub.

People who live in San Salvador may choose from a wide variety of entertainment. They can go to *El Teatro Nacional* ("The National Theatre") to see a play. If they want to dance, they can go to a nightclub or party where

Los Hermanos Flores ("The Flores Brothers") or *La Orquesta Casino* ("The Casino Orchestra") is playing. Luis Lopez, a popular performer, plays guitar and piano and sings. Salvadorans love to dance to his music. For those who prefer classical music, there are concerts by *La Orquesta Simfónica de El Salvador* ("The Symphonic Orchestra of El Salvador").

There are fewer places to go in the country and small towns, but that doesn't keep people from having fun. Parties at home, where people dance the *cúmbia*, are a common way to get together. If the town has a theater, movies are also popular. Salvadorans of all ages look forward to going to *el cine* ("the movies").

Whether they are out on the town for the night or visiting friends on a Sunday afternoon, most Salvadorans are relaxed about time. They don't schedule their days full of appointments, and often they don't have a sense of urgency about doing things, especially when it comes to social life. A Salvadoran shopkeeper wouldn't think of calling his mother on the phone before going to see her. Instead, he stops in at her house whenever he likes.

Families in Wartime

Families are one of the strongest bonds in Salvadoran culture. They are usually very large, often with

A Salvadoran mother, father, and child.

six or seven children in the family. Poor parents want their children to have a better, easier life than they had. They love their children very much and think of them as the hope for the future. That hope gives them the strength to keep on working even when they are extremely tired. Salvadorans work very hard, and most earn only enough money to feed their families.

The war in El Salvador has put a lot of strain on families. Families have been torn apart by deaths and disappearances and have been forced to leave their homes to escape from bombs and bullets. Thousands have left their country and have gone to Honduras, Mexico, or the United States. Sometimes a whole family travels together. At other times, a family is separated, and its members travel north alone. These Salvadorans don't want to leave their homeland, but they believe they don't have any other choice because they fear for their lives.

In certain parts of the country, people don't stay out late at night. They are afraid that they will be caught in gunfire. Since they no longer know whom they can trust, Salvadorans are forced to be more secretive than they used to be. They have to be very careful about what they say to anyone. If their message is misunderstood, they might be taken away by army soldiers and questioned or even killed. Many people are afraid to dress in mourning and visit cemeteries after friends or relatives have died because the government might link them to guerrilla activities.

Partly because of the war, the role of some women in El Salvador is changing. There are women who fight in the guerrilla army, and some of them are commanders. Many Salvadorans say that women should not carry guns and wear army uniforms.

Even though women in El Salvador have always worked, only certain types of work have been acceptable. As long as a woman works in the house and

Salvadoran women get up as early as five in the morning to fetch water for their families. Most Salvadorans do not have running water in their homes.

garden, makes tortillas, tends chickens and pigs, and washes clothes, she is doing work that is acceptable to her husband and to other men. She may also sell produce or tortillas at a market or work as a *doméstica* ("maid"). And during the coffee harvest, everyone has to work in the fields.

In the cities, women who are students and professionals don't accept this traditional way of thinking.

They believe women should do the work they want to do rather than the work men think they should do.

Most Salvadoran men, however, do not believe women are their equals. Especially in the country, the birth of a girl is still a disappointment to the father. He is happy and proud when a son is born.

A Changing Church

Besides the family, religion is another important bond in the Salvadoran culture. Most Salvadorans are Catholic, and only a small percentage go to Protestant churches. El Salvador has a Catholic church tradition that dates back to the time of the Spanish conquest. But not all Salvadoran Catholics attend mass regularly. Some Catholics attend church only twice in their lifetime—at their first communion and at their wedding.

To many Salvadorans, the Catholic church offers a tradition they grew up with, and one that they don't want to change. They like the quiet, solemn services which give them a chance to escape from the work and worries of daily life. Today, though, more and more people identify with the new Catholic church.

The Catholic church in El Salvador, and in all of Latin America, has changed a great deal in the past twenty years. In 1968 church leaders established a completely new focus for the church at a conference in

A shrine to the Virgin Mary in San Miguel.

Medellin, Colombia. They called it "liberation theology." When they returned home, these bishops and priests started to teach people the new theology, or system of religious beliefs. They used to preach that people must suffer poverty, hunger, and injustice on earth and await their reward in heaven. Now the church leaders tell peasants and workers that they must organize and act to change their situation here on earth.

Archbishop Romero

Archbishop Oscar Arnulfo Romero is one of the most famous and loved church leaders in El Salvador. Oscar Romero was born in 1917 in Ciudad Barrios in central El Salvador, where his family led a simple life. Romero's father was a telegraph operator in the isolated mountain village where they lived. Until Romero was twenty-three, the village could be reached only on foot or horseback. Then the first dirt road was built. At the age of thirteen, Romero apprenticed himself as a carpenter. Later he decided to become a priest and studied at the Gregorian University in Rome.

In 1977 Romero was made archbishop, the highest position in the Catholic church in El Salvador. At first Romero defended the coffee growers, the military, and the government leaders. But he changed his ideas when his friend and fellow priest, Retulio Grande, was assassinated for preaching liberation theology.

At this time the government and wealthy land-owners were suspicious that priests such as Retulio Grande were making the poor people restless. Several church leaders were tortured and killed for preaching liberation theology. Archbishop Romero was called "the voice of the voiceless" because he began to speak out for the people who had died or disappeared. "The church is not against the government," he used to say. "The truth is that the government is against the people and we are with the people."

During his Sunday morning mass at Metropolitan Cathedral in San Salvador, Archbishop Romero preached against violence. Hundreds of Salvadorans crowded the cathedral to hear his sermons. Thousands more across the country listened to mass over YSAX, the church's radio station. Although he was a powerful speaker, Archbishop Romero was a shy, thoughtful man who chose to live in a small room at a cancer hospital rather than keep a place of his own.

In earlier years as a parish priest, Romero used the church newspaper to criticize outspoken priests and defend the government. As archbishop, he used the same newspaper to list names of persons who were picked up off the streets or dragged out of their homes by the government security forces and who never returned.

On March 23, 1980, Archbishop Oscar Romero delivered his last sermon. In it he spoke directly to the Salvadoran people: "No soldier is obliged to obey an order against the will of God. . . .In the name of God and the name of this suffering people, I ask you, I beg you, I order you—stop the repression." While Romero celebrated a memorial mass, he was shot dead by an assassin who fired a single bullet through his heart.

More than 100,000 people attended his funeral, many of whom had traveled from across the country. At the funeral, gunfire showered the crowd gathered outside the cathedral. When it ended, close to sixty people lay dead or dying. The government said that the killings were the fault of the guerrillas. Religious leaders from around the world who attended the funeral claimed that the shooting came from the roof of the presidential palace. They think the government was responsible for the shooting. To this day, no one has been convicted for killing Archbishop Romero or anyone in the crowd. Archbishop Romero is dead, but he lives on in the hearts of his devoted followers. Each year they hold a religious service to mark the anniversary of his death.

Archbishop Romero demonstrated the power of language. Through his weekly sermons he gave people hope and strength and moved them to action. To help understand Salvadorans, we should look at their language.

Archbishop Romero's tomb in San Salvador.

A Poetic Language

Spanish is a Romance language, along with French and Italian. A Romance language has its origins in Latin, a language spoken in ancient Rome. Languages can tell us much about the people who speak them. Spanish is a poetic language, and to an outsider, it seems that everyone who grows up speaking Spanish should have been a poet!

Spoken Spanish is a flowing, gentle language. It has no harsh sounds which come from the throat. Instead, words are formed near the front of the mouth and seem to roll off the tongue. The *r* is the trickiest sound for non-Spanish speakers to make. A single *r* requires a simple, short roll of the tongue, while a double *r* requires a repeated roll of the tongue. Making this sound might take you a while to learn, but when you do you may find that it's great fun to use *r* words.

Just as we notice special features of the Spanish language, Salvadorans learning English point out some strange things about our language. In Spanish a human leg is a *pierna*. An animal leg is called a *pata*, and *pie* or *pata* is the word for a table leg. Salvadorans think it's odd that there is only one word for "leg" in English when there are so many different kinds of legs.

Several Salvadorans have used their language to write well-known poems and novels. Alfredo Espino, who lived from 1900 to 1928, is a dearly loved nature poet. Many Salvadorans can still recite *Las Manos de Mi Madre* ("My Mother's Hands"), a poem which they learned in school. Alberto Masferrer wrote novels in the early 1930s that often deal with human suffering and basic human rights.

Salvadorans have a special culture made up of peasant dances and weekly mass, large families and fine literature. But there is a big country to the north which influences Salvadoran culture. In the cities and the countryside, radios play music by bands from the United States, and many of the movies and TV programs are from the United States. A number of American companies do business in El Salvador. There are signs advertising U.S. soft drinks, baby food, electric appliances, gasoline, and much more throughout the country.

Some Salvadorans worry about this influence. They are afraid that their Mayan legends, Salvadoran music, and dances are being pushed aside to make room for television soap operas and fast-food restaurants from the United States. Because they are proud of their heritage, their Indian-Spanish background, and their customs, they want to preserve the Salvadoran culture for new generations of Salvadorans.

3. From Corn and Coffee to Revolution

The first people who lived in what is now El Salvador were Nahua Indians, who arrived from Mexico as early as 3000 B.C. Later, other Indians settled in this area. Most of the region we now call Central America was inhabited by the Maya Indians between A.D. 100 and 1000. The Pipíl tribe took control of the lands west of the Lempa River during the 1000s. During the next five hundred years, the Pipíl raised crops, built cities, and developed excellent skills as weavers.

The Indians were agricultural people who raised mostly corn, beans, and squash. Corn was their most important crop. The Indians called it "your grace" and thought it was the supreme gift of the gods. Planting and harvesting corn were so important to these ancient people that they took great care with their *milpas*. *Milpa* is the Indian word for a small corn field.

Because their survival depended upon their crops, the early Mayas learned a great deal about the seasons. They developed a calendar which is more accurate than the Roman calendar we use today. Their calendar aided them in planting and harvesting. It also guided them in their religious ceremonies, which they observed in order to please the gods.

Like the ancient Indians of El Salvador, these men and boys raise corn in carefully tended fields.

The Mayan year was made up of eighteen months of twenty days each, plus five extra days. The Mayas had no scientific way of measuring time—not even an hourglass—and no astronomical telescope. And yet, they tracked the planets with precision.

The Spanish Empire

The Indian world was disrupted in 1522 when the Spaniards invaded El Salvador. When the Indians saw

This limestone pyramid at Tazumal in western El Salvador was built by the Mayas between A.D. *100 and 1000.*

horses and shotguns for the first time, they were frightened. They thought the man-and-horse pair was some sort of god and that shotguns were magical instruments.

In 1524 Pedro de Alvarado attempted to conquer El Salvador and make it part of the Spanish empire. Instead of fighting the Spanish army, the Indians retreated to the rugged hills. After waiting seventeen days for the Indians to return, Alvarado gave up and returned to Guatemala.

The next year the Spaniards returned and made El Salvador a part of their empire. Before long, Indians were working for the Spaniards instead of for themselves.

El Salvador became very valuable to the Spanish empire when there was an international demand for cacao. Cacao is used to make chocolate. When the Spanish first tried chocolate, they didn't like it at all. It was not very sweet since the Indians made chocolate out of water, cacao, corn meal, and chile pepper. Once the Spanish added sugar to the recipe, chocolate became popular throughout Europe.

In the 1700s indigo was an important export crop. Indigo is a plant which is used to make blue dye. As Europeans started making more textiles, they needed more dyes. Almost all of the indigo they used came from El Salvador.

Independence

In 1821 El Salvador gained its independence from Spain. For one year the Central American countries united with Mexico, and then they formed their own union. The Central American Federation passed an antislavery resolution freeing black slaves, but it did little to benefit the Indians. Many Pipíl Indians were drafted to serve in the government army. Finally the Indians began to rebel about the way they were being treated.

In 1833 Anastasio Aquino led the first major Indian uprising in the vicinity of Santiago Nonualco, a traditional Pipíl area. Aquino's army of 4,000 men was easily defeated by the smaller, but better equipped, government army. Afterward Aquino escaped and lived in the surrounding hills for a couple of months. He was then captured and executed.

El Salvador became an independent nation when the Central American Federation disbanded in 1839. At the same time, El Salvador began producing coffee and shipping coffee beans to coffee-drinking countries all over the world. The land became so valuable that the *ejidos* ("common lands") the Indians farmed were taken away from them. Soon the rich coffee growers controlled almost all of the best farmland in big plantations called *fincas*.

Conditions for farm workers as well as city workers were very poor. They worked long days, sometimes fifteen hours at a time. Their pay was so low that they could seldom provide enough food for their families. In order to gain some rights, workers began to form unions in the 1920s. The unions guaranteed better wages and working conditions. When the government started prohibiting union rallies and strikes, a man named Augustín Farabundo Martí worked harder than ever to organize Indians in western El Salvador.

Martí and La Matanza

Martí was born to a wealthy landowner in 1893. At a young age, he worked for and understood the problems of the poor. He studied law at the National University, where he was known for challenging the things his professors said. Martí had to leave the university when he was arrested for demonstrating against a visiting Guatemalan dictator. He was sent to Guatemala as punishment. In Guatemala, Martí helped found the Central American Socialist Party, a group that struggled to gain basic rights for workers. Eventually he returned to El Salvador.

Martí once said that "when history can no longer be written with a pen, it must be written with a rifle." Since no real changes had taken place while he was away,

Martí led a peasant uprising in 1932. As many as 30,000 peasants, most of them Indians, were killed by government forces. People with Indian features and wearing peasant clothes were rounded up and shot even if they hadn't taken part in the rebellion. As a result, the Indian culture, language, and dress of El Salvador were almost destroyed. Because so many were killed, the battle is still called *La Matanza* ("The Massacre").

Paulina Patres, a survivor of La Matanza, remembered what it was like in a recent interview. "House by house they went. They took out the men and tied their hands. I told my father, 'Quick, hide, the soldiers are coming.' He told me, 'I have committed no crime, my daughter. I don't need to hide.' Well, I went inside and did some chores. Then they came to where my father was lying on a hammock, tied his hands, and took him out to the street and shot him. My father, my brother, and the father of my children, my husband. And then they just left them there, all dead."*

Martí was put to death by the administration of Martínez, the general of the army and president of the country. Because the modern-day guerrillas agree with the things Martí fought for, he is their hero. The guerrilla army is called the FMLN, which stands for Farabundo Martí Liberation Front.

Before, during, and after Farabundo Martí's lifetime, El Salvador has had a long line of military govern-

*See note in Selected Bibliography.

ments. A military government doesn't separate the army from the government. Often the president of the country is also the general of the army. If there are two leaders, one the president and the other the general, the general usually has control over everything the president does. In most cases one person has complete power.

General Martínez, who ordered La Matanza, ruled longer than any other Salvadoran president. Like General Martínez, earlier and later presidents didn't do much to help the poor.

Duarte and the Christian Democrats

In the 1960s a new political party was formed to improve conditions for workers and poor people. José Napoleón Duarte was the first member of this party to be elected mayor of San Salvador. Duarte had studied engineering at Notre Dame University in the United States. When he returned to El Salvador, he married into a wealthy family. Elected mayor of San Salvador in 1964, Duarte was a popular mayor because of his personality as well as his politics. He forced the rich to pay the taxes they owed, built new markets, and provided street lights and garbage collection. No previous mayor had done such things. Duarte was reelected twice.

In 1969 the progress of this new party was inter-

rupted by a war between El Salvador and Honduras. It is known as the "Soccer War" because it broke out soon after the World Cup playoff matches between the two countries. The real cause of the war, though, was the border between El Salvador and Honduras. Its exact location had always been in question, and people from either country were frequently captured near the border. After a month-long war, Salvadoran troops began to withdraw from Honduras. By this time, 3,000 people had died.

Three years after the Soccer War, Duarte decided to run for president because everyone thought he had the best chance of winning. El Salvador's military leaders also believed that Duarte would win. But when the election was held and the ballots were counted, the government announced that its candidates had won. Duarte and his supporters accused the military leaders of rigging the election. Then, without warning, the government arrested and tortured Duarte and sent him to Venezuela. He lived there until 1979, when he returned to El Salvador.

In that same year, a council made up of two military and three civilian leaders took over the Salvadoran government. The two army officers in the council did not trust the three political leaders from outside the military. Before long the civilian leaders left the government because they could not make the changes that they

José Napoleón Duarte, president of El Salvador.

felt were needed in Salvadoran society. After they left, the army officers asked members of the Christian Democratic Party—led by Duarte—to join the council.

In 1980, the new government took over many of El Salvador's largest farms and seized control of the country's banks and foreign trade. Then it began to distribute some of the farmland to poor people. Soon, however, it became clear that this land reform program would not work. The wealthy landowners and military death squads threatened to kill any peasants who dared to move onto the farmland. By the early 1980s, Duarte and the Christian Democrats were caught in the middle of a civil war between the army and the guerrillas.

Some of his old supporters felt that Duarte had changed his ideas while he was in Venezuela. They felt that he was favoring the wealthy now and that his arrest and torture made him afraid to stand up for the workers and the poor. Whatever he had lost, Duarte still wanted to lead his country. He was asked to serve in the government and became president in 1983. In 1984 and 1985 his Christian Democratic Party won national elections.

After he had returned to El Salvador and joined its government, Duarte talked about his reasons for trying to work with Salvadoran military leaders. He discussed the conditions in El Salvador during the civil war. "The values of life have been lost. People just kill because of killing. They could get by with it because there was no protection, no police. That was the situation. This was when they called me. . . .The most difficult thing was to accept the challenge to correct that. This is what I did."*

Duarte was elected while his country was at war. Some Salvadorans say that he was elected unfairly because the voting wasn't done honestly. They claim that the voting was rigged by the government, just as it had been in most previous elections. Other Salvadorans say that it is impossible to have meaningful elections when a country is at war. They believe that in order to have a democracy, a country must do more than have elections. It must also have court trials when innocent people are taken out of their homes and killed.

The U.S. government supports President Duarte and El Salvador's army. It sends money and military aid to the Salvadoran government to help the Salvadoran army in its battle against the guerrillas. "The national security of all the Americas is at stake in Central America," said President Reagan in April 1983. "If we cannot defend ourselves there, we cannot expect to prevail elsewhere." The U.S. government claims that the guerrillas get their arms and training from the Soviet Union, Cuba, and other Communist countries. Improvements in Salvadoran society can be made, say U.S. officials, with Duarte as president.

Most Salvadorans, however, live in constant terror of the government army. They claim that the death

*See note in Selected Bibliography.

squads which kill and torture their friends and relatives
are in most cases the soldiers of El Salvador's military.
So far, the dangers they must face in their daily life have
not changed because Duarte is president.

Fighting for Change

The guerrillas don't believe that the lives of most
Salvadorans will improve with Duarte as president. In
1980, the FMLN was formed because the guerrillas
didn't think change could take place peacefully.

Ruben Zamora was one of the Salvadoran leaders
who joined together to form the FMLN. Along with
other Salvadoran leaders in this group, he had tried to
work for peaceful change in the 1970s. In 1979 Zamora
served for a short time in the Salvadoran government,
but left when he found that he could not work with the
military leaders. Recently Zamora gave his view of the
reasons for the civil war and the decision of the FMLN
to fight for change in El Salvador.

"If we are struggling now politically and militarily,
it is not because we like weapons. It is because we have
tried everything. We tried political parties. We tried
elections. We tried street demonstrations. We even tried
an alliance with the military through a military coup.
And the problem was always that there could be no
democracy—there could be no change. There was resis-

Men and women from different classes and backgrounds have become FMLN guerrillas.

tance to change. We did not invent armed struggle in El Salvador. We arrived at it after every other alternative failed."*

The guerrillas in the FMLN are fighting for a new society in El Salvador, one that they believe would be more fair and more respectful of human rights. In order to force the government into a position of economic hardship, they have blown up buses and bridges. The guerrillas have kidnapped and killed a well-known member of the government and a wealthy landowner. Promi-

*See note in Selected Bibliography.

A guerrilla stands beside a brightly colored FMLN banner.

nent FMLN leaders such as Ruben Zamora live in exile in Nicaragua.

The FMLN is made up of university professors, ex-government officials, army deserters, doctors, priests, and peasants. Salvadorans call the guerrillas *los muchachos* ("the boys"). But there are many women in the guerrilla army as well. The best known woman in the FMLN was Ana Guadalupe Martínez, a medical student who left school to join the guerrilla army. She was killed in 1983.

Not all people who agree with the guerrillas fight

with them. One example is the Committee of Mothers and Family Members of the Assassinated and Disappeared. This group of 500 members was formed in 1977. Each member has lost at least one family member because of the war and believes the government is responsible for her loss. The group holds demonstrations and marches in San Salvador and pleads with the government officials to tell them where their missing relatives are. Few are ever given any information.

Women from the Committee of Mothers and Family Members of the Assassinated and Disappeared march in San Salvador.

Although President Duarte and the guerrilla leaders had a few face-to-face meetings in 1984, not much was accomplished. Each side makes demands that the other side refuses to meet. When neither side is willing to compromise, it is difficult to make any progress toward peace.

Several Central American poets have compared the circumstances behind the revolution in El Salvador to the activity of the volcanoes that dot the landscape. Even though a volcano doesn't erupt constantly, write the poets, it can erupt at any given time if the conditions are right. The same is true, say the poets, of poor people whose living conditions and basic human rights never improve. They rebel now and then until the time is right to start a full-scale revolution. The rebellions of 1833 and 1932 were minor eruptions compared to the revolution being fought today.

For the people of El Salvador, recent years have been a time of danger, sadness, and change. Peaceful change may still be possible if the government and the guerrillas can agree to work together. For now, though, El Salvador remains a place of beauty among the ashes of war.

4. *The Devil Made Me Do It*

An old Mayan legend tells about the beginning of the human race. First the gods made a human being out of wood, but the wooden person could not speak with the gods. Since the gods were not pleased with what they had done, they sent a flood. Next the gods made a human like an animal, with a voice. When they found out that this person could not act with reason, the gods sent another flood. Four times the gods did not care for the creatures they had created, and four times they sent a flood. Finally, the gods made a human from a golden kernel of corn and were pleased.

A different legend explains the Mayan view of the world. The Mayas thought of the world as flat and square and suspended between thirteen heavens and underworlds, all of them ruled by gods. A huge ceiba tree stood at the center of the earth. Smaller trees were located at the four corners, and each corner was paired with a color. White went with north, yellow with south, red with east, and black with west. A god ruled each corner and color, and a bird of the right color nested in the trees at the corners of the earth. The world rested on the back of a huge crocodile which floated in a special lily pond.

The Oral Tradition

Every country has a tradition of folktales and legends. Many of them began long before there was a written language. Legends give meaning to things in life that we cannot otherwise understand. The story about a human being created from a kernel of corn helped early Salvadorans understand their own beginning. The legend about the Mayan view of the world helped the Mayas understand the world around them. Without these legends, they would have felt lost in their own world.

Not all legends, though, are old ones. New legends are created all the time for many different reasons. They help us understand the world, but they also help us to enjoy the world. Salvadorans, like people everywhere, enjoy a good story.

In a country such as El Salvador, folktales and sayings remain an important part of the culture. Perhaps that is because many Salvadorans cannot read and write. El Salvador has a long history of oral tradition— the telling of stories from one generation to the next. It's a special library that exists in the heads of people rather than in the books in a public building.

Instead of reading their children a bedtime story, Salvadoran parents and grandparents tell a story they remember from their childhood. But in the telling and retelling, a story can change. Someone might forget an

While she works, a Salvadoran mother tells a story to her daughter.

incident, and someone else might add one. There are also regional differences in Salvadoran folktales. While the same themes and stories show up in all parts of the country, there are minor differences from place to place.

Speaking of the Devil

In many folktales the devil is a central figure. The devil's temptations are to be avoided at all costs or you will lose your soul, the folktales say. In fact, some poor people believe that rich people have sold their soul to the devil in order to become rich.

The *Justo Juez de la Noche* ("The Just Judge of the Night") is a story about the devil. The Justo Juez is a tall man who wears a black suit. No one has seen his face, but his eyes are like fire. He appears only at midnight, and mostly to people traveling alone in rural areas.

A man named Julio was walking alone one night when he saw a very tall man in his path. The two men walked and talked together for several hours. Then, very suddenly, the Justo Juez took out his machete and tried to strike Julio. But Julio was experienced with the machete and managed to strike the Justo Juez. The Justo Juez just laughed when he was hit, and he didn't bleed or get hurt. His laugh was so loud that it could be heard many miles away. When Julio looked at the face of the Justo Juez and saw the red eyes, he ran away as fast as he could. Eventually Julio went crazy because he didn't want to make a pact with the devil.

Another story about deceptive appearances—about things not being what they seem—is the story of *La Siguanaba*. The character of La Siguanaba also appears to travelers, but not necessarily at night. She lives near the river. La Siguanaba is an ugly, old woman who can turn into a beautiful, young woman at will. She usually approaches a man traveling alone and asks for a ride. Since she is very beautiful, the man falls in love with her and gives her a ride. After they have been riding together for a while, the beautiful, young woman who has been flirting with the man suddenly turns into an ugly, old woman. She has hair to the ground, backwards feet, and very long fingernails. Some people say that La Siguanaba also has hairy hands and frozen skin. The man gets so frightened that he runs away, gets sick, and sometimes even dies of fright.

La Siguanaba has a child named the *Cipitio*. The Cipitio is a little boy with brown skin and a bloated belly from not eating enough of the right food. He doesn't wear any clothes except for a big hat called a sombrero. The Cipitio doesn't scare people like his mother does, for he is an innocent child who lives and plays in the river. Still, people don't like him because they don't like his mother.

The story of the *Cadejos*—another story with the

devil in it—is about a good spirit and a bad spirit. The *Cadejo* is an imaginary animal that looks something like a dog. The *Cadejo Blanco* ("White Cadejo") is the good Cadejo, and he protects people who travel during the night. The *Cadejo Negro* ("Black Cadejo") is evil because he is a follower of the devil. Since the Cadejo Blanco tries to protect the traveler whom the Cadejo Negro is trying to harm, the two Cadejos are enemies.

At first, the Cadejo Negro is friendly and affectionate to a traveler. But if you talk to him, he tries to win you over to the devil by using his magical powers. And if he wins you over, you lose your soul to the devil. People who talk to the Cadejo Negro are said to disappear forever.

Magic and Witchcraft

In El Salvador, some people believe in *brujería*. Brujería is witchcraft, or magic, and it is an Indian tradition. Today, not everyone believes in this kind of magic. But in certain parts of the country, especially remote rural areas, people believe in brujería. In the town of Izalco there are centers where witchcraft is practiced. People from other provinces visit these centers if they have problems with illness or with love that they think magic can cure. The person who practices brujería is called a *curandero*.

A Salvadoran mother may call a curandero to her house if her newborn baby is sick. She is afraid that someone who recently visited her newborn child had sight so strong that he hurt the baby. In order to make sure that no harm was done when this person made eye contact with the baby, the mother asked him to hold the child. But if he admired the child from a distance and didn't hold it, he may have harmed the child. Then, the mother believes, the baby will get sick immediately.

In that case, the curandero comes to the house and has the baby chew garlic until it is a fine paste. She rubs the garlic paste on the child's body, puts a garlic necklace on the child, and says prayers. Next she holds an egg up to the sun. If the egg has a small circle in the top of the white part, that means the child has been harmed by the visitor's strong sight, just as the mother suspected. The curandero then puts the egg in a bowl and continues treatment until she is certain she has cured the baby.

Curanderos sometimes help people with problems of love, too. If a girl loves a boy who doesn't pay any attention to her, she can go to the curandero for help. The curandero will put magical scented powders on the girl's wrist. After the girl sees the boy she loves three more times, greets him, and shakes his hand, he will fall in love with her. The boy has no control over his feelings for her; the powders have made him fall in love.

If a husband leaves his wife and children without any money, his wife may go to the curandero for help in finding him. The curandero smokes a cigar during the woman's visit. While he smokes, he can tell the woman everything she wants to know about her husband's whereabouts. Then the curandero smokes two more cigars and says some prayers. At that point, he can tell the woman exactly when and where her husband will return.

Salvadoran Sayings

Salvadoran folklore is made up of more than stories and legends and brujería. There are Salvadoran sayings about everyday kinds of things, such as good and bad luck. If you sweep the floor at night, you are supposed to have bad luck. Your mother is supposed to die.

In order to have good luck, say some Salvadorans, you are supposed to look at the morning star. If you look directly at the morning star when it goes up at night and when it goes down in the morning, you will have very good luck.

Legends and folktales, magic and sayings—all are part of the Salvadoran oral tradition and culture.

5. A Good Time for Everyone

Certain dates on the Salvadoran calendar are marked with a big star. Throughout the year, there are many holidays and celebrations. Salvadorans look forward to those times when ordinary days are made special, when a meal includes good meat, and when getting dressed means putting on an attractive outfit. Because El Salvador is a Christian nation, the most important holidays its people celebrate are Christmas and Easter.

Christmas Cheer

Christmas is called *La Navidad* ("The Nativity"), and the Christmas season can start as early as mid-December. In some towns children carry out a tradition called *posadas* ("inns"). Posadas are parades which re-enact the travels of Mary and Joseph before Jesus was born. The children walk from house to house carrying images of Mary and Joseph, and at each house they stop to have something to eat. They also sing to the *nacimientos*, which are the figures in the nativity scene.

In El Salvador, large, indoor nativity scenes are more common than Christmas trees, but trees are becoming more popular. Salvadorans use two different

kinds of Christmas trees. They can buy artificial trees that look like pine trees, or they can decorate a small, bare branch, which looks something like a tumbleweed until it is decorated.

Marta's family starts the Christmas season on December 20 by going to San Salvador to shop for new clothes. Although her family doesn't have much money, everyone manages to find an inexpensive outfit in the market. This year Marta buys a new blue dress, and she is so proud of it that she can hardly wait until the twenty-fourth to wear it. She worked hard in order to get her new dress. While harvesting coffee all fall, her mother would tell her to hurry up and work faster so that she would make enough money for a new Christmas outfit.

On December 24, Marta's family wears the new clothes to evening mass at the church. Christmas Eve mass is special and very beautiful. Everyone sings Christmas carols, and there is a pageant in which Marta dresses as Mary and her younger brother David dresses as a shepherd. After mass Marta's family visits friends and eats tamales, beans, bread, and chicken. They dance and talk all evening until it's time to go home to bed.

The next morning—Christmas morning—Marta wakes up to find a whistle made of clay under her pillow. She blows her new whistle, and the noise wakes up David. Under his pillow there is a little plastic car.

At Christmastime Salvadorans often decorate their homes and churches with nacimientos—*the figures in a nativity scene.*

The children are pleased by their gifts from *El Niño Dios* ("Baby Jesus"). Marta and David spend most of Christmas Day outside in the street with their friends, playing with their new toys and those of their friends.

The Easter Season

The Easter season begins with Ash Wednesday, the first day of Lent. Many Salvadorans go to mass on Ash Wednesday because it's a tradition, and others go because they have deep religious beliefs. For faithful Salvadoran Christians, Lent—the forty weekdays before Easter—is the most religious time of the year.

The week before Easter, called *Semana Santa* ("Holy Week"), begins with Palm Sunday. People walk to Palm Sunday mass carrying flowers and palm branches. Several communities usually have mass together since there isn't a priest in every community. During this special mass guitars accompany the people in a musical celebration of Jesus' entry into Jerusalem.

During Holy Week most Salvadorans eat meals of fish instead of beef and pork in memory of Jesus' suffering on the cross. Fish scrambled in egg is a favorite dish during Holy Week. No one cooks on Thursday, Friday, and Saturday morning because Christians are mourning the death of Jesus. On Thursday the Last Supper is observed at mass. Twelve men are selected to have their feet washed by the priest, in the same way that Jesus washed the disciples' feet.

On Good Friday the procession of Jesus and the cross takes place. Four people carry the image of Jesus and the cross through town and sing songs that recall his suffering. During Holy Week Archbishop Romero and others who died in the war are also remembered in song and prayer. When the procession arrives at the church at noon, four more people arrive with an image of Jesus nailed to the cross. In Izalco the image of the crucified Jesus is so large that it takes seventy-five people to carry it. The people in the procession dress in the clothing of Jesus' day.

Many Salvadorans feel that this is the time at which the message of Holy Week becomes real. The suffering of Jesus is something the people, especially the poor people, understand. The civil war has brought about so much suffering that Salvadorans believe they are living Lent in a real way through their everyday experiences.

After the Good Friday procession, people go home to eat, or visit a friend. It is a serious, quiet day, and parents don't allow their children to play much. Since Judas ran when he betrayed Jesus, children aren't supposed to run. Throughout El Salvador, in memory of Jesus carrying the cross to Calvary, few people travel. In a church ceremony at three o'clock, the image of Jesus is taken down from the cross. The people at the church wrap the image in white sheets and stand watchful with candles until it's dark outside. In the past they stayed at the church all night, but being outside in the dark is too dangerous while the war is going on.

On Saturday everyone sleeps late. In the afternoon most Salvadorans go to the nearest ocean beach or river and take along a picnic of corn tamales, watermelon, tortillas, and beans. At the Saturday evening mass, the people gather around a big bonfire outside the church. The priest lights a candle from the bonfire, and the people light their candles from the priest's candle. They enter the church carrying their candles, which represent Jesus before the resurrection.

On *Pascua* ("Easter Sunday") Salvadorans march in a joyous procession with an image of the risen Jesus and a blessing with water. Some people even bring their animals to have them blessed. After Easter mass, Holy Week and the sacred celebrations come to an end.

Saints' Days and Other Holidays

Since most Salvadorans are Catholic, saints play a big part in celebrations all year long. The patron saint of the country is *El Salvador del Mundo* ("The Savior of the World"), whose day is celebrated on August 6. People from all parts of the surrounding province travel to San Salvador for the celebration of El Salvador del

In El Salvador, a patron saint's day is a time for Catholics to march through the streets in celebration.

Mundo. Part of the fun is a big *feria* ("fair") with a circus, amusement park, and vendors selling special foods.

Each city also has a patron saint of the Catholic church, and once a year that city celebrates the day of its saint. Patron Saints' days are busy, fun-filled times. In fact, Saints' days usually last a whole week! Soccer teams compete in tournaments, people dance in the streets, and sometimes the circus comes to town. During all these exciting events there are parades and processions in which the image of the saint is carried around the city.

Patron Saints' Days are exciting for the young women who hope to be chosen *Reyna* ("Queen") of the Patron Saints. People in the community buy tickets in order to vote for their favorite candidate. The candidate who receives the most votes becomes the queen.

Not all Salvadoran holidays are religious ones. On New Year's Eve the whole family stays up very late, eating, dancing, and visiting with friends. On this night Salvadorans often sing a song called "Five to Twelve" and another one called "*Feliz Navidad*," a popular Christmas song by José Feliciano. At midnight the church bells ring, and people bang on pans, light firecrackers, or shoot guns to make a lot of noise. Everyone runs out into the street to hug other people and say, "*Feliz Año Nuevo*" ("Happy New Year"). Even if someone is mad at her neighbor, she will forget about it on New Year's Eve.

Some celebrations take place in only one city or part of the country. The city of San Miguel, for instance, has a huge carnival every year. The San Miguel carnival used to be called a marimba festival because most of the music was provided by people playing marimbas. Now, though, the music is provided by orchestras and dance bands which set up along the main streets of the town. During the carnival, there are as many as twenty bands in a space of twelve blocks! The streets are packed with people, which makes it impossible to walk quickly. All day and night the bands play and people dance in the streets until they are so exhausted that they go home to bed.

El Quince de septiembre ("The Fifteenth of September") is a holiday that is observed throughout El Salvador and Central America. On this date in 1821, Central America gained its independence from Spain. In El Salvador, schoolchildren observe the whole week, called *La Semana Cívica* ("Civic Week"). They paint pictures of the leaders of independence, and the schools have special programs honoring these heroes in which the children sing national anthems and songs. On the fifteenth school bands and elementary schoolchildren march in the streets. The military also has a big parade that features army tanks driving through the streets and helicopters flying overhead. For many Salvadorans family outings and picnics are popular on Independence Day.

The family is included in almost all holidays and celebrations in El Salvador, and Mother's Day is an especially big day. Children usually remember to buy a simple gift for their mothers, but if they forget they can count on their teachers to remind them. Even if sons or daughters live in another city, they try to visit their mother on Mother's Day.

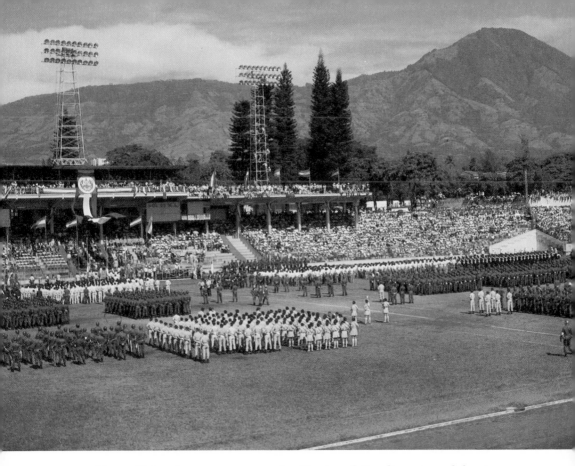

Many Salvadorans come to the National Stadium to celebrate Independence Day, September 15.

Special Celebrations

While some days are celebrated by all Salvadorans, other days are special for only one or two people. A birthday is one example. Children in El Salvador have big birthday parties for their friends in which they dance and eat sandwiches and cake. Sometimes they break a *piñata*. A piñata is a papier-mâché figure, often shaped like an animal, which hangs from the ceiling. Blind-folded children take turns striking at the piñata with sticks. When the piñata breaks, the candy inside of it falls to the floor. Then everyone goes after the candy in a mad scramble!

Another important day for most Salvadoran children is First Communion. On this day they receive Holy Communion at Catholic mass for the first time. Children in El Salvador usually celebrate their First Communion when they are eight or nine. If their families have enough money, girls wear fancy, white dresses, and boys wear new outfits, too.

The first important church occasion for most Salvadoran children is baptism. If it's performed in a church, many children are often baptized at the same time. Sometimes the baptism is performed at home, with only the priest, the baby's family, and the *padrinos* ("godparents") in attendance. The godparents feel a responsibility to help care for their godchildren and try to give them money or a gift on special occasions.

A Salvadoran Wedding

When they grow up, young Salvadorans look forward to celebrating their marriage. Salvadoran couples can have any kind of wedding they like. Some brides wear a long white dress and veil, but many brides either can't afford to buy a bridal gown or choose to have a simple wedding. The wedding usually takes place in a

Catholic church. If the families involved are wealthy, they will have a fancy reception afterwards.

In communities without a regular priest, couples have to wait for a visiting priest to make a trip to marry them. When he arrives, many couples will get married in the same ceremony. In one remote village, Archbishop Romero once conducted a wedding in which thirty couples got married at the same ceremony!

Jorge remembers the first wedding he attended. The wedding was held at the church, with almost the whole community in attendance. The bride wore a yellow, street-length dress and carried a bouquet of wildflowers. The groom wore his best trousers and a white, long-sleeved shirt. The bride and groom didn't exchange gold rings because they couldn't afford them. Instead, they tied a piece of ribbon around each other's finger. The priest had told them that spending money on rings would be foolish since they needed the money for food and clothing. He told them that what mattered most was that they loved each other.

After the ceremony, everyone in the community brought food to the party. Jorge ate tamales and drank lemonade and *horchata*, a drink made from ground corn and water. The dance was held outside, under a roof fashioned from tree branches. All night long the band, made up of an accordion, guitar, and string bass, played *ranchera* music. A ranchera is a Mexican dance.

The bride and groom danced the first dance, and then everyone joined in the fun.

Whether the occasion for celebration is a patron saint's day or a wedding, Salvadorans can count on some things to be the same. There will be plenty of food and dancing, and a good time for everyone.

6. Salvadoran Homes and Food

Pase adelante. ("Come in.") This is how you would be greeted if you were visiting a Salvadoran home. You would be offered a chair, perhaps one of the only chairs in the house, and you would be given something to eat or drink. Then the family members would gather around you to visit and ask questions. If you could speak Spanish, you would begin to carry on a conversation with them.

You would soon find out that a household in El Salvador usually includes more than a mother, father, and children. It is common for grandparents to live with a family, and sometimes aunts and uncles and cousins move in, too. Since there are no nursing homes in El Salvador, the family must care for old relatives. You might see a grandmother and her grandson feeding the chickens together or an aunt babysitting for her niece. Together they make up a Salvadoran family and household.

A Salvadoran household is not quite complete unless it includes a dog or two. Salvadorans like dogs for companionship and protection. Many people believe that dogs are more like humans or gods than they are like animals, and that dogs have souls. They feed stray dogs as if they were their own. If the dog belongs to them, they give it lots of love and affection. Dogs don't always live in the house, but they know which family they belong to, just the same.

Since the homes of poor Salvadorans are usually small, they are often crowded. Most of these homes have only one or two rooms. Sometimes there are curtains instead of walls separating one room from the next. At night, everyone pulls out cots and mats or settles into hammocks if there aren't enough beds to go around.

Small children play on the porch of a typical house in the Salvadoran countryside.

In rural areas homes made of straw thatch, called chozas, *are common. These homes do not have electricity or running water.*

In the rural areas, homes made of straw thatch, called *chozas*, are common. Only the more well-to-do families in the country can afford white-washed adobe homes. Although rural houses usually have dirt floors and just a few pieces of furniture, most have pictures of one or more saints or holy figures on the walls. Homes of poor people seldom have electricity or running water. Kerosene lamps or candles provide light at night, and water is carried from the nearest well or stream.

A Mother's Work

The *mamá* ("mother") of the household gets up very early in the morning to fetch the water and put it on to boil. She gathers firewood for the fire, which is lit on a raised platform oven called an *ornilla*. Then she starts making tortillas for her family. The hard, ripe kernels of corn are first soaked or boiled in a mixture of water and white lime, which makes a kind of paste or dough. Next the mamá grinds the dough on a *metate* ("grinding stone") with a *mano* ("handstone"). Later she slaps the dough into tortillas. Since she does this almost every day, she is very quick and good at making tortillas. As she works, the dough makes a "pat, pat, pat" sound between her hands. When the tortillas are ready to be cooked, she toasts them on a *camal* ("clay griddle") above the fire.

Many women make more tortillas than their family can eat. They take the extras to the *mercado* ("market") in hopes of earning a few *colónes*—Salvadoran money.

A Salvadoran market is a feast for the eyes, ears, and nose. Colorful flowers, fruits, and vegetables overflow from baskets and onto tables. The smell of flowers, fresh tortillas, and tamales greets shoppers long before they get to the market. Early in the morning, when most women do their shopping, the market is filled with the sound of people bartering.

A Salvadoran girl toasts tortillas on a camal *("clay griddle") above a cooking fire.*

Bartering goes something like this. A customer approaches the vendor selling tomatoes and asks how much they cost. The vendor quotes a price. The customer says that she won't pay that much, offers a lower price, and starts to walk away. Afraid that she will lose business, the vendor then offers a price halfway between her offer and the customer's offer. That way the vendor makes a sale, the customer gets her tomatoes, and both are happy.

Women carry their purchases in wicker baskets or string bags which they bring with them to the markets. When they are young, they learn to carry a wicker basket filled with produce on their heads. By the time they grow up, they can walk very gracefully with a heavy load balanced on their heads.

In small towns markets are often found in the main plaza. In larger cities they are sometimes housed in buildings. Women go to the market early in the morning before the best produce is sold.

Many people come to shop for food every day at this busy market in San Salvador.

If the mother of the household doesn't go to the market, she works hard at home. She cleans the house, prepares lunch and dinner, and carries dirty clothes to the nearest river to scrub them against the rocks. The clean clothes are left on the rocks to dry. The mother also feeds the chickens and pigs, milks the cow, and works in the garden. If it is harvest season, she works with the men in the fields.

Poor city women often work in factories or as maids, and men also work in factories. Many Salvadorans, though, don't have full-time work. Unemployment is a big problem in El Salvador.

Men and Machismo

Men in rural El Salvador often have to work away from home, sometimes traveling many miles to find seasonal work. The men think of themselves as heads of the house, even if they are away from home for months at a time. In some cases fathers don't have much to do with their families, and seldom or never live at home.

Machismo is the word that describes the attitudes of many Salvadoran men. It means that they think they are more important and smarter than women and has to do with the pride men have about being men. Often Salvadoran women also believe that men are smarter and more important than women are.

Whether or not they have these attitudes, almost all Salvadoran men want to have children. Couples in El Salvador start having families at a young age. In fact, many women have their first child when they are as young as fourteen or fifteen. Each woman gives birth to many children during her lifetime. Yet because of poor nutrition and poor medical care, almost half of the children in El Salvador die before they are five years old. Perhaps six or seven children from a family of ten or twelve will live to adulthood.

The marchers in this funeral procession carry the casket of a young Salvadoran child.

A Salvadoran mother and her children work together at home.

The children who survive must grow up quickly in order to help their family earn a living. Seven-year-old children sometimes work alongside their parents in the fields.

Not all Salvadoran couples get married officially. It is common for a man and woman to live together and raise a family without having a legal wedding. Such an arrangement is called a "common law" marriage because society recognizes that the couple wants to live together.

Wealthy Salvadorans

Almost all middle- and upper-class Salvadorans have a legal marriage. These people have plenty of money, and they lead very different lives than those of poor Salvadorans. For one thing, wealthier Salvadorans have more leisure time than poor Salvadorans do. The women do little work unless they work outside the home. Each household has at least one maid, and often two or more, to do the housework. One maid might be in charge of cooking, another will clean, and a third will do the laundry or take care of the children.

In their spare time, well-to-do Salvadoran women shop at fancy clothing stores and buy their groceries at modern supermarkets. They keep track of styles from the United States and Europe and live more like United States and European women than like the poor women in their own country. The very rich think of themselves as European in manner and Salvadoran only by birth.

Middle-class men work in offices as doctors, accountants, lawyers, teachers, and businessmen. The wealthy landowners, called the oligarchy, don't actually go to work every day. Since these men have other people do their work, they simply oversee the operation from time to time. They visit their coffee fincas to make sure that everything is running smoothly.

Unlike poor Salvadorans, the wealthy own cars and

don't have to depend on public transportation. Owning
a car in El Salvador is quite a luxury. In the countryside
people must walk, ride a mule or a horse-drawn cart, or
take the bus. Rural Salvadorans think nothing of walking five or ten miles to get to town. If a rural Salvadoran
is ill, he or she has to be carried on a stretcher made of a
hammock slung between branches. There are no roads
to many remote villages, which are called *aldeas*. The
bigger towns, called *pueblos*, usually have bus service,
and here live chickens are often taken to the market on
the bus. In the Salvadoran countryside, a bus has to be
an all-purpose vehicle!

Although daily life in El Salvador usually moves
along quite quickly, there is a time set aside each day for
rest. A *siesta* is a one- or one-and-a-half-hour break in
the day when people have lunch and take naps or relax.
Shops close down from noon until one or half-past one
in the afternoon. Especially in the hottest parts of the
country, people need to take a break from the heat
during that time of the day.

Salvadoran Meals and Foods

When Salvadorans come home for siesta, it's time
for *almuerzo* ("lunch"), the biggest meal of the day. For
desayuno ("breakfast") it's common to have a diced hot
tortilla in fresh, warm milk or a hot, salted tortilla and

coffee. Since most people eat breakfast between six and eight in the morning, they're hungry again by noon. For their big meal, they may have soup, tortillas, rice, and cheese or some kind of meat. *La cena* ("supper") is a small meal eaten between half-past four and five which usually consists of tortillas and beans.

Salvadoran meals vary somewhat from one part of the country—and from one class—to another. Seafood is much easier to come by in the south than it is in the north, for instance, and rich people eat differently from poor people. Wealthy Salvadorans eat meat every day and buy more prepared foods. Poor people, on the other hand, don't have much variety in their diet. Still, certain foods seem to be popular in homes in the north and south, and among the rich and the poor.

Papusas are just one example. Papusas are tortillas with an extra ingredient cooked into the center. Melted cheese is a common stuffing for papusas, but shredded pork or mashed beans is sometimes used, too. The smell of a warm papusa with melted cheese inside gives just about everyone an appetite.

Salvadoran beans are red. To prepare for eating, they are boiled until they soften, and then fried in oil. The leftover beans are put in a clay pot and fried again for the next meal or the next day. That's why they're called refried beans, or *frijoles refritos*. They improve with age by taking on more flavor the longer they sit in

A farm family shares a meal.

the clay pot. (See the recipe on pages 89-90.)

Strangely enough, most Salvadorans don't drink good quality coffee because the best coffee in the country is shipped to other countries. Most people make their own coffee, either from corn or from the bark of the coffee tree. If coffee is made from coffee beans, it usually comes from poor quality beans that have shells and dirt on them. When it's served with milk, though, the coffee tastes fine. The milk makes the strong drink milder, and easier on the stomach.

Many Salvadoran foods aren't easy for us to prepare. For instance, we sometimes don't have the correct utensils or the right ingredients, and few people have the skills to make tortillas.

The three recipes given below can be made without very much work. Ask your mom or dad to help you make one of these recipes.

Aguacate ("Guacamole")

1 avocado, peeled and diced
1 hard boiled egg, diced
1 large ripe tomato, diced
1 tablespoon lime juice
1/4 teaspoon Worcestershire sauce

Mix ingredients. Add salt and pepper to taste. Serve with tortilla chips for an appetizer or snack.

Frijoles Refritos ("Refried Beans")

1 pound pinto beans, red or black
4 tablespoons lard
2 cloves garlic, chopped
1 large onion, chopped
4 cups boiling chicken stock
salt to taste
1/2 cup lard
1/4 cup grated monterrey jack cheese (optional)

Frijoles Refritos (continued)

Soak beans in water for 8 hours or overnight. Drain off water. In large cooking pot, melt 4 tablespoons lard. Add garlic and onions. Stir continuously until garlic is golden and onion is transparent. Add drained beans to garlic and onion mixture and stir to coat the beans with the fat. Add enough boiling chicken stock to cover beans. Stir once more and bring to a boil. Cover, reduce the heat to very low and simmer, stirring from time to time to be sure beans won't stick to the bottom of the pot. If beans absorb all the liquid before they are done, add more chicken stock (but be sure to heat it to boiling). Simmer for 4 hours, stirring occasionally. When done, season with salt to taste and let cook for 10 minutes more. Drain beans, saving the liquid.

In a large skillet, melt 1/2 cup lard. Add some of the beans to the hot fat and mash thoroughly. Keep adding more beans and mashing; then add some of the liquid and more beans until all of the beans and liquid are used. Keep stirring and cooking until mashed bean mixture is thick and dry. If desired, top with grated monterrey jack cheese. Makes 6 servings.

Ensalada ("Salad")

1/2 head cabbage, chopped fine
6 radishes, chopped fine
4 tomatoes, chopped fine
2 cucumbers, chopped fine
2 carrots, chopped fine
2 tablespoons lime juice

Toss the vegetables together with the lime juice and serve in a large bowl.

Now, call your family to the table and say "*Buen provecho.*" In El Salvador that means "good appetite" or "enjoy your meal!"

7. School Days in Wartime

When the morning school bell rings, Salvadoran children race to the center of the school yard and get in line. They stand still while their teachers walk down the rows. The teachers look for neatness—shined shoes, neat uniforms, and combed hair. Then the students sing the national anthem and hear announcements from the principal. When *formación* ("formation") ends, the young people run inside to their classrooms.

Most children in El Salvador start school, but not many finish more than three or four grades. Sometimes they quit school because they have to work. At other times their parents can't afford the uniforms and book bags that most schools require. And now, because of the war, thousands of Salvadoran children don't attend school because the schools are closed. Several hundred teachers have been killed, and several hundred others have fled El Salvador because they feared for their lives. In at least one instance, a school has been closed and is being used as an army post.

Despite the war, many children still attend school. Their days are filled with math problems and verb conjugations, and their evenings are filled with homework.

Two Salvadoran schoolgirls, dressed in their school uniforms, are interested in the book they are reading.

Teresa's School Day

Teresa's school is on the edge of the town where she lives. Every morning she walks to school wearing a white blouse, plaid skirt, white stockings, and black shoes. Teresa carries her books in a book bag called a *bolsone*. Girls carry their books in a bookbag while boys carry their books in a backpack.

As Teresa approaches the school, she can hear her classmates playing in the school yard. The school is made up of three long buildings in a row, with a soccer field at one end. Teresa walks fast because she doesn't want to be late for formación. She arrives just in time, waves to her friend Luisa, and gets in line with her classmates.

After formación Teresa and her third grade classmates go to their room and wait for their teacher. When Señorita López walks in, she says "*Buenas días, clase.*" ("Good morning, class.") "*Buenas días, Señorita López,*" the class responds. Then Señorita López takes roll. When she says "Teresa Rivera," Teresa stands and says "*presente*" ("present").

Math—Teresa's favorite subject—is the first class of the day. Since her class is large (there are forty-five students in one room) and because there are not enough books to go around, each student shares a book with a math partner. Today Teresa is called on to demonstrate a multiplication problem on the blackboard. Señorita López compliments her for doing it correctly and continues with the lesson.

Each class period lasts one hour. After the first period, there is a short recess when the students go outside to play and buy mangoes or candies from the nearest vendor. When recess is over, it's time for social science. Since the third graders are learning about their country, Señorita López calls fourteen students to the front of the class. Each of them represents one of the departments, or provinces, of El Salvador. She asks them, one at a time, to name the capital of their department, the major rivers and lakes, and several other places and geographic features of their country.

The last two classes of the day are Spanish grammar and natural science. In grammar class the students practice verb conjugations. Señorita López says *"comer"* ("to eat"), and the class responds: *"como"* ("I eat"); *"comes"* ("you eat"); *"come"* ("he/she eats"); *"comemos"* ("we eat"); *"comen"* ("they eat"). The students continue with harder verbs and then work on spelling.

Science class is spent discussing various kinds of trees found in El Salvador. When the clock strikes twelve and the bell rings, Teresa stuffs her books in her bolsone. But she doesn't leave before Señorita López says *"Deberes, clase"* ("Homework, class") and quickly writes a homework assignment on the blackboard. Te-

In a Salvadoran schoolroom, two boys write in their notebooks.

resa copies the assignment in her notebook and then runs home.

Teresa's mother has prepared a big lunch of soup, tortillas, chicken, and rice. Since Teresa is very hungry, she sets the table quickly. After lunch and a short nap, she goes to her friend Luisa's house to meet with her study group.

Everyone in Teresa's class belongs to a study group made up of twelve to fifteen students. Study groups prepare for the final exams given at the end of October.

All Salvadoran students take final exams at the end of the school year, and the third graders will be tested on the four classes they have. Students who don't pass the final exam have to repeat the grade. This afternoon Teresa's study group decides to work on spelling.

Trying Times for Teachers

While Teresa's study group meets, another class of third graders sits in Señorita López's classroom. Because Salvadoran schools do not have enough teachers, books, and buildings, they run on a split-shift schedule. The morning shift goes from 8:00 until 12:00, and the afternoon shift lasts from 1:00 until 5:00. Several students in the afternoon classes had to leave home at 9:00 in the morning in order to get to school by 1:00. They live up in the mountains where there are no schools. When they walk home at the end of the day, it is dark most of the way. They usually bring their dogs along with them for company and to help them along the dark path.

Some boys and girls can't go to school during the day because they have to do farm work. A small number of these young people are able to go to school in the evening. They get home late at night and have to get up the next morning to work in the fields again.

Salvadoran teachers work very hard but don't get paid much. Before the war some of them belonged to a teacher's union called ANDES. Since then, however, many members of that union have been killed, and others have fled the country.

The Salvadoran government has set up a common schedule of coursework for students all over the country, but because of the war it is especially difficult for teachers to follow it. The school year runs from the end of January until the end of October, with a one-week break for Holy Week. In first grade, students learn about the county or city where they live. In second grade, they learn about their province, and in the third grade about their country. Fourth grade deals with Central America, fifth grade with the Western Hemisphere, and sixth grade the whole world.

In private schools there are enough materials and teachers so that the required set of courses can be followed. Most private schools in El Salvador are run by the Catholic church. Since parents have to pay tuition for students in private schools, only well-to-do families can afford to send their children there. In addition to their regular classes, private school students have opportunies to join music groups and sports teams.

High School and College

Almost all private school students go on to junior and senior high, and many of them graduate from

Salvadoran schoolgirls share a happy moment.

college. Junior high and senior high schools in El Salvador are often divided into schools for boys and schools for girls. At the junior and senior high level, Salvadoran students study from twelve to fifteen subjects throughout the school year. In seventh grade they start studying English, a language that most young Salvadorans find difficult to learn.

After ninth grade, students can study for their *bachillerato* ("degree"). If a young man wants to be a bookkeeper, he studies for the bookkeeping bachillerato. There are few jobs, though, for students who graduate with secretarial or bookkeeping skills. In fact, many graduates have to do unskilled work in a factory even though they are qualified to do skilled work. If a student wants to go to the university, he or she studies for the academic bachillerato.

There are two universities in El Salvador. The National University of El Salvador is a public university. It has been closed many times because the government thinks it is a center of guerrilla activity. In 1984 the National University opened again, but it is no longer a center of academic freedom. Several books that the government thinks teach Communist ideas have been removed from the library. If professors are not careful about what they teach, they may be removed from their position. The Central American University of José Simeón Cañas, or *UCA*, is a private university. Students have to pay tuition in order to attend this university.

For the average Salvadoran, the chances of attending a university are extremely limited. Less than half of the people in the country can read and write, and libraries and books of any kind are scarce. In order to get any education at all, there are serious obstacles to overcome.

Tomás's Story

Tomás started the first grade when he was seven. Because his family was poor, it took a great deal of effort for him to finish primary school. In first grade Tomás didn't have shoes. He had to wear patched shorts instead of long pants, and he had only one shirt. He carried a thin notebook and a pencil in a plastic bag. During recess, when most of his classmates were outside playing, Tomás stayed inside to study. He wanted to learn as much as he could since he hoped to go to the university some day.

When Tomás was in third grade, he had to work during the day. He hoed tobacco and earned money equal to twenty-five U.S. cents for fifteen hours of work. At night Tomás went to school. When he was working, he could buy himself a pair of shoes and a pair of long pants.

Tomás didn't have the opportunity to attend secondary school because the war caused his school to close. Now he reads books at the priest's library and picks up any dirty piece of paper he sees on the street, just to practice his reading. Tomás would like to return to school some day, but he doesn't know when that will be possible.

8. Salvadoran Sports and Fun

On a Sunday afternoon in almost any Salvadoran town, a group of young boys will be playing soccer, and girls will be playing softball. Soccer, which is called *fútbol* in Spanish, is the most popular sport in El Salvador. As soon as little boys learn to run, they practice running while kicking a soccer ball. If they don't have a ball, they pretend they are kicking one while they run down the street.

If a group of neighborhood friends doesn't have enough money to buy a ball, the boys make one. They each bring a bunch of rags from home and then choose someone to take a used nylon stocking from their mother or older sister. They stick the rags in the stocking and roll it into a ball. If they decide they want to play with a real ball, they charge each player five centavos and go out and buy a ball.

Boys from wealthier families play with a real soccer ball and often join teams at their schools or in their neighborhoods. When they grow up, they want more than anything to be chosen for the *Selección Nacional* ("National Selection"). The National Selection is a team made up of the best high school and university soccer players and represents El Salvador in international com-

*Boys have fun playing a pickup game of soccer on the main
street of a small town.*

petition. Salvadorans love to watch the National Selection play teams from other countries. If the team plays in San Salvador, soccer fans buy tickets so that they can cheer for their team in the National Stadium. Many others watch the game on television or listen to it on the radio.

Salvadoran TV

Watching television is a popular form of recreation in El Salvador, even though most people don't own a set. The country has three commercial and two educational television stations, but has no national programs. Almost all of the shows on Salvadoran TV are from the United States. "Magnum P.I.," "General Hospital," "The Dukes of Hazzard," "Bonanza," and "The Bionic Woman" are popular shows. Young children like to watch "Tom and Jerry," "Popeye," and "Smurfs." The programs are dubbed in Spanish, which means that the voices of English-speaking actors are replaced with the voices of Spanish-speaking actors.

Most people in the rural areas don't have a television because few poor people can afford to buy one. But if someone does buy a television, he or she has to be prepared to share it with the neighbors. As soon as a television arrives in the neighborhood, people will line up to ask if they can watch it. Sometimes the owner's house or apartment gets so crowded that the first arrivals have to leave in order to make room for the new arrivals! Some owners charge ten centavos to let their neighbors watch a show. That way, they can pay for the television more quickly.

Fun and Games

Since most Salvadorans don't have much money, the most popular sports and forms of recreation are those that don't require any special equipment. Toys and books of any kind are scarce. Often toys are made of sticks, tin cans, or whatever happens to be lying around.

Some Salvadoran children don't have much time to play. Children who work in the fields are often too tired to play at the end of a long working day. After they have been picking coffee for ten hours, playing games doesn't seem like much fun.

But when they are in the mood to play, they can think of plenty of games which don't require any equipment. Salvadoran children like to play *mica*, or tag. Another kind of tag is called *ladrón librado* ("freed thief"). Ten or more people can play this game. Some are thieves, and others are police officers. The police try to catch the thieves, and when they do, they take them to an electric pole or tree and guard them. If another thief comes by and says "ladrón librado," the thieves are free to go. They run away, and the police try to catch them once again. Everybody would rather be a thief instead of a police officer because the police spend all their time chasing thieves. It's more fun to run away.

Although few Salvadoran children learn to swim, most like to go to the nearest river whenever they get a chance. Rural children go to the river when their mothers do laundry.

Miguel remembers running along the water with his dog while his mother scrubbed clothes on the rocks and

A Salvadoran mother washes clothes in a stream while her child plays in the water.

laid them out to dry. If there was a big pile of laundry, they would take a basket of tortillas and beans along for lunch. Miguel enjoyed spending the day at the river, but he dreaded his mother's call just before they were ready to leave. She would call him to remind him to bathe.

When Miguel bathed himself, he rubbed a little soap on his stomach, rinsed it off, and considered himself clean. But his mother said that if he didn't bathe well he was sure to get lice. She would start at the top of his head and scrub him thoroughly with a huge bar of strong soap. Miguel hated the smell of the strong soap and hated getting soap in his eyes. He thought the dog was lucky, because even though the dog had fleas, it didn't have to bathe with soap. At the end of the day, Miguel and his mother walked home with the dog running alongside.

Going To Town

Walking is one of the most common forms of exercise in El Salvador. For many Salvadorans, walking is the only way to travel from their homes to where they want to go. On Sunday mornings people from the rural areas and small villages walk to the nearest town to spend the day. Early in the morning they go to the market and in the afternoon the adults visit with friends in the central plaza. The children play nearby.

In the center of every Salvadoran town there is a square park called a plaza. The plaza is filled with trees, shrubs, and flowers. A sidewalk forming a square runs along the edge of each side of the plaza, and a sidewalk forming an *X* crosses the middle. There are benches beside the sidewalk, and sometimes a fountain or small tower in the middle of the plaza. A person can sit here for hours on end, just reading the newspaper, watching people, or daydreaming. Shoeshine boys set up business along one side of the plaza, and paper boys and food vendors try to sell their products to passersby. Although it looks like the center of activity, the plaza is a place where most people come to relax.

Salvadorans of all ages get together to have fun. An evening in a small town is a likely time to have a party where everyone is welcome. Instead of splitting into groups according to age, with each group going its separate way, people from three to seventy-three will spend the evening together. Almost every good party will include dancing.

When Salvadorans dance to Latin music, they dance the cúmbia, *salsa*, or ranchera. Sometimes they dance to rock-and-roll songs, but most people prefer Salvadoran music. Salvadoran children start dancing soon after they can walk. They dance with their parents, their friends, and if there aren't enough partners to go around, they dance by themselves!

In the countryside of El Salvador, people do a lot of walking.

9. Strangers in a Strange Land

Most Salvadorans who have come to the United States have done so since 1979. In almost all cases, they have left their homeland because of the civil war. While Salvadorans live throughout the United States, most have settled in the South and Southwest, especially in Miami, New Orleans, Los Angeles, and cities in Texas and Arizona. Los Angeles has the second largest Salvadoran population of any city in the world! Immigration officials estimate that 250,000 Salvadorans live in Los Angeles. Only San Salvador is home to more Salvadorans.

Most leave El Salvador because their lives are in danger, because members of their family have been killed or tortured, or because friends have disappeared. Some people are allowed to leave El Salvador legally. These fortunate Salvadorans have a passport and a visa and can travel by airplane. Most, however, do not get permission to leave their country. Their decision to leave is often made in a hurry. In most cases, because they have to be secretive, they can bring only a few clothes and a little money in their bags. Sometimes they don't even have the chance to tell their friends and family good-bye.

A Long, Hard Journey

The trip is long and hard. It is common for Salvadorans to travel in crowded vans or trucks. Others travel alone, and walk or hitchhike part of the way. First they have to cross Honduras, then Guatemala and Mexico, and at last they arrive in the United States. Not everyone goes that far. In fact, many Salvadorans stay in Honduras and Mexico. Honduras and Mexico have refugee camps that were set up to provide food and shelter for Salvadoran refugees of the war.

For those who continue on to the United States, the United States-Mexico border is the most difficult one to cross without a passport or visa. Immigration officials patrol the land with cars and jeeps, and the air is filled with helicopters, all trying to prevent illegal border crossings. Still, many Salvadorans cross the border without getting caught.

They can cross it alone or they can hire a "coyote" to help them cross the border. A coyote is a guide who helps people without passports or visas cross the border. He usually charges about two hundred dollars to help a Salvadoran cross the United States-Mexico border. If the coyote has traveled all the way from El Salvador with a refugee, he might charge anywhere from a thousand to three thousand dollars. Most people hire a coyote because he knows the best paths and the best

Salvadoran children in a refugee camp in El Salvador. These children have lost their parents during the civil war.

times of day to cross the border without getting caught.

For many Salvadorans Los Angeles is the first stop in the United States. As many as 90 to 150 Salvadorans arrive in Los Angeles every day! A Salvadoran refugee center called *El Rescate* ("The Refuge") helps the new arrivals. El Rescate is funded with donations, mainly from churches in the Los Angeles area. The center helps Salvadorans adjust to life in a foreign land by trying to find them work and a place to live. Everything is different in the United States—the language, the food, the people, the prices, and the lifestyle. Many refugees suffer from homesickness and loneliness. Often they had to leave their family behind in El Salvador.

The Life of a Refugee

Salvadorans in the United States are seeking refuge, which is the reason they are called refugees. Most Salvadorans who are here without a visa don't intend to live in the United States for the rest of their lives. They are not immigrants in the same way that some of our grandparents and great-grandparents were immigrants. These Salvadorans only want to stay here until they believe that it is safe to return to El Salvador. Until that time comes, they want to be granted asylum by the U.S. government. When a government grants asylum to people from another country, it is providing them with shelter during a time of great danger in that country.

The U.S. government does not grant permanent or temporary residence status to most Salvadorans because it says that they are here for economic reasons rather than political reasons. Salvadoran refugees want good jobs, says the government, and they came to the United States in order to improve their income. The refugees say that they came because there is a war in El Salvador and that they were running for their lives when they left their country.

Only a few out of every hundred Salvadoran refugees are granted asylum in the United States. If they have marks on their bodies to prove that they have been tortured in El Salvador, they will probably be allowed to remain. Sometimes written pleas from their family in El Salvador will help get them asylum.

Salvadorans who do not get residence permits usually live in a Hispanic community in a city such as Los Angeles. These refugees live alongside Mexicans, Guatemalans, and U.S. citizens of Latin American heritage. They read Spanish newspapers, listen to Spanish radio and television, and eat beans, tortillas, and rice. And yet, there are plenty of reminders that they are in the United States instead of El Salvador.

For one thing, Salvadoran refugees have to be very careful not to get caught by U.S. immigration agents. If they are stopped and the agents discover that they don't have official refugee status, they will be deported, or sent back, to El Salvador. Immigration agents frequently conduct raids of factories and restaurants where they expect to find a large number of Salvadoran workers.

Even though most Salvadorans don't have the legal right to work in the United States, many companies and individuals are willing to hire them. Salvadorans without a work permit will work for less money than United States citizens, which is why certain companies and individuals will give them work. Many of them work as maids or farm laborers, doing the same kind of work they did in El Salvador.

Seeking Sanctuary

For Salvadorans who do not get official permission to live in the United States, there is a program called sanctuary. Sanctuary is a network of about two hundred Protestant and Catholic churches throughout the country that provides shelter for illegal refugees from El Salvador and Guatemala. The sanctuary movement was started by the Reverend John Fife of Tucson, Arizona, in March 1982, because he did not want United States immigration agents to return Salvadoran refugees to their country. Fife said that returning Salvadorans to El Salvador was sending them back to be tortured or killed.

The people involved in the sanctuary network know that it is against the law to aid illegal refugees. They believe in following God's law, which says they should help their brothers and sisters in need. Because they think that United States policy toward Salvadorans is unjust, these church members follow their religious beliefs instead of their country's law. Several of these U.S. citizens have been arrested, and some have been found guilty of helping to transport or house Salvadoran refugees.

Some refugees live in the churches which provide them with sanctuary, while others live in a family home. When they appear in public, they often wear sunglasses, or a bandana over most of their face, so that they won't be recognized. They don't want to reveal their identity because they are afraid that their families back in El Salvador will be punished by the military or death squads.

Many sanctuary refugees feel that they must tell their story to make people in the United States aware of what is happening to their country. The refugees claim that the money the United States sends to El Salvador is used to support an unjust government and military. They ask U.S. citizens to write to Congress and the president and tell them to stop sending money to the government and military in El Salvador.

Not all Salvadoran refugees want the U.S. government to stop supporting the government of El Salvador. There are some privileged Salvadorans in the United States who left their country for different reasons than most other refugees. These rich Salvadorans are worried that they may be kidnapped or killed by the guerrilla army. Most of them have homes in Miami or New Orleans where they are now living. They worry that they will lose their money and their land or businesses if the government does not win the war in El Salvador.

Five Stories

Some Salvadorans came to the United States before the war began in their homeland. Guillermo de Paz is a Salvadoran who came to the United States in 1974. He studied at the University of Minnesota and received his degree there. Just before he was going to return to his home in San Salvador, he received word that his brother had been killed by the death squads. Instead of returning to El Salvador, Guillermo started political organizing in the Midwest. He meets with various Central American political groups and speaks at conferences, meetings, and demonstrations throughout the country. In 1984 Guillermo was appointed the FMLN spokesperson for the Midwest.

Emerson Figueroa came to the United States under quite different circumstances. Figueroa was a professor of law at the National University of El Salvador. He was also a member of the Human Rights Commission, which was formed in 1977 with Archbishop Romero's support. Figueroa volunteered to help this commission, which spoke out against human rights abuses in El Salvador. Many members of the commission have been kidnapped and killed by the death squads. Figueroa came to the United States because his life was in great danger. He has been given permission to live in the United States, and he now teaches at the University of Iowa. Since he worries that his family in El Salvador would be tortured or killed if his identity were known, he doesn't reveal his real name.

Alicia Zelayandía came to the United States in 1980 because many members of her family had disappeared or had been killed in El Salvador. For thirty-seven years she taught in El Salvador. During that time she founded a private school in San Miguel and was also a founder of ANDES, a teacher's union. Zelayandía has permission to live in the United Staes. From her home in San Francisco, she travels throughout the United States to give speeches about the terrible things going on in her native country. She says that the government and the military are harming, not helping, the people of El Salvador.

Yadira Arevalo is a Salvadoran refugee who has been sheltered by the sanctuary movement in Duluth,

Minnesota. Yadira fled to the United States in 1980, at age sixteen, after she received a threat from a death squad. Because she was teaching adults to read and write in her church, the death squads thought of her as a Communist threat. Arevalo would like to return to El Salvador some day so that she can continue her studies in her own country. She had been in high school for only six months when she had to leave El Salvador. Arevalo dreams of being a professor at the university when she finishes her studies.

René Hurtado is a refugee who had been given sanctuary by a church in a suburb of Minneapolis, Minnesota, until he was arrested by U.S. Immigration and Naturalization Service agents. He is now in jail and will soon face trial. At that time the courts will decide if Hurtado can remain in the United States, or if he will be deported to El Salvador. Hurtado was a member of the treasury police in the Salvadoran armed forces before he fled to the United States. As a refugee he gave public speeches about the torture done by the military in El Salvador.

An Uncertain Future

It is hard to say when Salvadorans by the thousands will quit fleeing to the United States. As long as they feel unsafe in their homes and schools and on their streets

and soccer fields, they will continue to leave their homeland. Until the war is over, many Salvadorans will stay in the refugee camps in Honduras and Mexico and in the Hispanic communities and sanctuary churches in the United States.

Salvadorans everywhere look forward to a time when their country is again united. Although it is impossible to know when the war will end or what the outcome will be, one thing is certain. The people from a country with provinces named *La Paz* ("Peace"), *La Libertad* ("Liberty"), and *La Unión* ("Unity") do want peace, liberty, and unity for future generations of Salvadorans.

Yadira Arevalo, a Salvadoran refugee living in the United States, hopes she can be a professor in El Salvador someday.

Appendix A

Salvadoran Consulates in the United States and Canada

Salvadoran consulates in the United States and Canada offer assistance to Americans and Canadians who want to understand Salvadoran ways. For information and resource materials about El Salvador, contact the consulate or embassy nearest you.

U. S. Consulates and Embassy

Houston, Texas
Consulate General of El Salvador
6655 Hillcroft Street
Suite 112
Houston, Texas 77081
Phone (713) 270-6239

Los Angeles, California
Consulate General of El Salvador
408 S. Spring Street 608
Los Angeles, California 90013
Phone (213) 680-4343

Miami, Florida
Consulate General of El Salvador
150 SE 3rd Avenue
Suite 520
Miami, Florida 33131
Phone (305) 371-8850

New Orleans, Louisiana
Consulate General of El Salvador
1136 International Trade Mart
New Orleans, Louisiana 70130
Phone (504) 522-4266

New York, New York
Consulate General of El Salvador
46 Park Avenue
New York, New York 10016
Phone (212) 889-3608

San Francisco, California
Consulate General of El Salvador
870 Market Street
Suite 721
San Francisco, California 94102
Phone (415) 781-7924

Washington, D.C.
Salvadoran Embassy
Consulate General of El Salvador
2308 California St. NW
Washington, D.C. 20008
Phone (202) 265-3480

Canadian Consulates and Embassy

Montreal, Quebec
 Consulate General of El Salvador
 370 St. Joseph Blvd. E.
 Montreal, Quebec H2T 1J6
 Phone (514) 842-7053
Ottawa, Ontario
 Salvadoran Embassy
 Consulate General of El Salvador
 294 Albert Street
 Suite 302
 Ottawa, Ontario K1P 6E6
 Phone (613) 238-2939
Vancouver, British Columbia
 Consulate of El Salvador
 1200 Burrard Street
 Suite 606
 Vancouver, British Columbia
  V6Z 2C7
 Phone (604) 681-1434

Appendix B
Say It in Spanish!

English Word(s)	Spanish Word(s)	Pronunciation
hello	*hola*	(OH-luh)
good-bye	*adiós*	(ah-dee-OHS)
yes	*sí*	(SEE)
no	*no*	(NOH)
good morning	*buenas días*	(BWAY-nuhs DEE-uhs)
good night	*buenas noches*	(BWAY-nuhs NOH-chays)
thank you	*gracias*	(GRAH-see-uhs)
please	*por favor*	(PAW fuh-VAWR)
excuse me	*perdóneme*	(pair-DOH-nay-may)
what do you want?	*qué quieres?*	(KAY kee-AIR-ays)
how are you?	*cómo estás?*	(COH-moh es-TAHS)
Mr.	*Señor*	(sehn-YAWR)
Mrs.	*Señora*	(sehn-YAWR-uh)
Miss	*Señorita*	(sehn-yawr-EE-tuh)
Ms.	*Seña*	(SEHN-yuh)

Spanish Adjectives

English Word	Masculine Form	Feminine Form
good	*bueno* (BWAY-noh)	*buena* (BWAY-nuh)
bad	*malo* (MAH-loh)	*mala* (MAH-luh)
pretty	*bonito* (boh-NEE-toh)	*bonita* (boh-NEE-tuh)
ugly	*feo* (FAY-oh)	*fea* (FAY-uh)
big	*grande* (GRAHN-day)	*grande* (GRAHN-day)
small	*pequeño* (peh-KEN-yoh)	*pequeña* (peh-KEN-yuh)

Spanish Names

Name	Pronunciation
Marta	(MAHR-tuh)
David	(dah-VEED)
Jorge	(HAWR-hay)
Teresa	(teh-RAY-suh)
Luisa	(loo-EE-suh)
Tomás	(toh-MAHS)
Miguel	(mee-GEHL)

Glossary

aguacate (ahg-wuh-KAH-tay)—guacamole, a dip made from avocado

aldeas (ahl-DAY-uhs)—small, remote villages

almuerzo (ahim-WAIR-soh)—lunch

bachillerato (bah-chee-ur-AH-toh)—degree; baccalaureate

bolsone (bohl-SOH-nay)—book bag

brujería (broo-hair-EE-uh)—witchcraft, or magic

Buenas días (BWAY-nuhs DEE-uhs)—"Good day"

Buen provecho (BWEN proh-VAY-choh)—"Good appetite," or "Enjoy your meal"

Cadejo Blanco (kuh-DAY-hoh BLAHN-koh)—"White Cadejo"; the good spirit in the folktale of the Cadejos

Cadejo Negro (kuh-DAY-hoh NAY-groh)—"Black Cadejo"; the bad spirit in the folktale of the Cadejos

camál (kuh-MAHL)—a clay griddle used for making tortillas

la cena (lah SAY-nuh)—supper

chozas (CHOH-suhs)—houses made of straw thatch

el cine (ehl SEE-nay)—the movies

Cipitio (see-pee-TEE-oh)—"Cipitio," legendary son of the Siguanaba

clase (KLAH-say)—class

colónes (koh-LOH-nays)—Salvadoran paper money

colonias (koh-LOH-nee-uhs)—suburbs

comer (koh-MAIR)—"to eat"

cúmbia (KOOM-bee-uh)—the name of a dance

curandero (koo-rahn-DAIR-oh)—witch doctor

deberes (day-BAI-rays)—homework

desayuno (dehs-y-OO-noh)—breakfast

doméstica (doh-MEHS-tih-kuh)—maid

ejidos (ay-HEE-dohs)—common land

ensalada (ehn-sah-LAH-duh)—salad

Feliz Año Nuevo (fay-LEES AHN-yoh NWAY-voh)— "Happy New Year"

Feliz Navidad (fay-LEES nah-vee-DAHD)—"Merry Christmas"

feria (FAIR-ee-uh)—fair

fincas (FIHN-kuhs)—big farms

formación (fawr-mah-see-OHN)—"formation," the assembly at the beginning of a school day

frijoles refritos (FREE-hoh-lays ray-FREE-tohs)—refried beans

fútbol (FOOT-bohl)—soccer

horchata (awr-CHAH-tuh)—a drink made from ground corn and water

Justo Juez de la Noche (HOO-stoh HWEZ day lah NOH-chay)—"Just Judge of the Night," a folktale

ladrón librado (lah-DROHN lee-BRAH-doh)—"freed thief," a game of tag involving police and thieves

mamá (mah-MAH)—mother

mano (MAH-noh)—a handstone used for making tortillas

El Mar de Lava (EHL MAHR day LAH-vuh)—"The Sea of Lava," a huge stretch of lava rock between San Salvador and Santa Ana

La Matanza (Lah muh-TAHN-suh)—"The Massacre"; the battle in 1932, led by Farabundo Martí, in which as many as 30,000 peasants were killed

mercado (mair-KAH-doh)—market

metate (meh-TAH-tay)—a grinding stone used for making tortillas

mica (MEE-kuh)—"monkey," the name for a game of tag

milpa (MIHL-puh)—a small corn field

los muchachos (LOHS moo-CHAH-chohs)—"the boys," a Salvadoran term for the guerrillas

nacimientos (nah-see-mee-EHN-tohs)—figures in the nativity scene

La Navidad (Lah nah-vee-DAHD)—Christmas

El Niño Dios (EHL NEEN-yoh dee-OHS)—"Baby Jesus"; children receive gifts from Baby Jesus at Christmas

ornilla (awr-NEE-uh)—oven

padrinos (pah-DREE-nohs)—godparents

papusas (pah-POO-suhs)—tortillas with cheese, shredded pork, or mashed beans cooked inside

Parque Infantíl (PAHR-kay ihn-fahn-TIHL)—"Children's Park," an amusement park in San Salvador

Pascua (PAHS-kwuh)—Easter

Pase adelante (PAH-say ah-day-LAHN-tay)—"Come in"

pata (PAH-tuh)—a table leg or animal leg

pie (pee-AY)—a table leg

pierna (pee-AIR-nuh)—a human leg

piñata (pihn-YAH-tuh)—a papier-mâché figure with candy inside, which children try to break at birthday parties

posadas (poh-SAH-duhs)—"inns"; the name given to parades before Christmas in which children reenact the travels of Mary and Joseph

presente (pray-SEHN-tay)—present

pueblos (poo—EHB-lohs)—towns

El Quince de septiembre (EHL KEEN-say day sehptee-EHM-bray)—"The Fifteenth of September," Independence Day

ranchera (rahn-CHAIR-uh)—a Mexican dance

El Reloj de Flores (EHL ray-LOH day FLAWR-ays)—"The Clock of Flowers," a giant clock made out of flowers in San Salvador

El Rescate (EHL rehs-KAH-tay)—"The Refuge," a refugee center in Los Angeles which helps many newly arrived Salvadorans adjust to American life

reyna (RAY-nuh)—queen

Río Lempa (REE-oh LEHMP-uh)—Lempa River

El Salvador del Mundo (EHL SAL-vuh-dawr del MOON-doh)—"The Savior of the World," the patron saint of El Salvador

Selección Nacional (sehl-ehx-ee-OHN nah-see-oh-NAHL)—"National Selection," the Salvadoran soccer team which plays in international competition

La Semana Cívica (LAH say-MAH-nuh SIH-vih-kuh)—"Civic Week," the week prior to The Fifteenth of September, Independence Day

Semana Santa (say-MAH-nuh SAHN-tuh)—"Holy Week," the week leading up to Easter

siesta (see-EHS-tuh)—an afternoon nap

La Siguanaba (LAH sihg-wuh-NAH-buh)—"The Siguanaba," a folktale

El Teatro Nacional (EHL tay-AH-troh nah-see-oh-NAHL)—"The National Theatre," located in San Salvador

temporales (tehm-poh-RAHL-ays)—heavy rains

tugurios (too-GOO-ree-ohs)—slums

Valle de las Hamacas (VY-yay day LAHS hah-MAH-kuhs)—"Valley of the Hammocks," the series of hills and valleys surrounding San Salvador

Selected Bibliography

Argueta, Manlio. *One Day of Life*. New York: Vintage Books, 1983.

Armstrong, Robert, and Shenk, Janet. *El Salvador: The Face of Revolution*. Boston: South End Press, 1982.

Arnson, Cynthia, *El Salvador: A Revolution Confronts the United States*. Washington, DC: Institute for Policy Studies, 1982.

Barry, Tom; Wood, Beth; and Preusch, Deb. *Dollars and Dictators: A Guide to Central America*. New York: Grove Press, 1983.

"Battle for El Salvador," from "Frontline," Part IV of "A Crisis in Central America." A production of WGBH Boston in association with the Blackwell Corporation for "Frontline."*

Bonner, Raymond. *Weakness and Deceit: U.S. Policy and El Salvador*. New York: Times Books, 1984.

"Central America: What U.S. Educators Need to Know." *Interracial Books for Children Bulletin*. Vol. 13, Nos. 2-3, New York: 1982.

Cheney, Glenn Alan. *El Salvador: Country in Crisis*. New York: Franklin Watts, 1982.

El Salvador: Background to the Crisis. CAMINO (Cen-

---

*Quotations in the text marked by asterisks are taken from "Frontline: Battle for El Salvador."

tral America Information Office). Cambridge, Massachusetts: 1982.

Gallenkamp, Charles. *Maya: The Riddle and Rediscovery of a Lost Civilization.* New York: David McKay Company, 1976.

Lernoux, Penny. *Cry of the People: The Struggle for Human Rights in Latin America.* New York: Penguin Books, 1982.

Montgomery, Tommie Sue. *Revolution in El Salvador: Origins and Evolution.* Boulder, Colorado: Westview Press, 1982.

Russell, Philip. *El Salvador in Crisis.* Austin, Texas: Colorado River Press, 1984.

Volcán: Poems from El Salvador, Guatemala, Honduras, Nicaragua. San Francisco: City Lights Books, 1983.

Index

About the Author

Faith Adams is a free-lance writer whose work has appeared in a variety of publications. On a trip to Central America in 1980, she conducted an independent study of *Amas de Casa*, a women's organization. Her experience in Central America led her to study and write about the people in that area of the world.

"This book makes the everyday and the ordinary events in the lives of Salvadorans important," says the author. "I have included significant people and events in El Salvador, but primarily in order to provide a clearer understanding of their effect on ordinary Salvadoran people. I hope that this book will make the reader curious to learn more about El Salvador and that the reader will gain an appreciation for Salvadorans everywhere and in every circumstance."

Ms. Adams's educational background includes a bachelor's degree in English from Saint Olaf College in Northfield, Minnesota. Currently she resides in Minneapolis.